By Dean Murray

Reflections

Broken

Torn

Splintered

Intrusion

Numb

Trapped

Forsaken

Riven

Driven

Lost

Marked

Left

Dark Reflections

Bound

Hunted

Ambushed

Shattered

Burned

The Awakening

Reborn

Immortal

Endless

A Broken World

The Society

The Destroyer

The Warlord

The Founder

The Desolation

Reflections

(Dean Writing as Eldon)

The Greater Darkness

A Darkness Mirrored

The Compelled Chronicles

Stone Heart

The Guadel Chronicles

Frozen Prospects

Thawed Fortunes

I'rone

Brittle Bonds

Shattered Ties

Splintered

Intrusion

Scent of Tears

Numb

Dean Murray

Splintered, Intrusion, The Scent of Tears and *Numb* are all works of fiction. Names, characters, places and incidents are the products of the author's imagination or are used fictitiously. Any resemblance to actual events, locales, or persons, living or dead, is entirely coincidental.

Published by Fir'shan Publishing

ISBN 978-1-9393631-1-4

www.FirshanPublishing.com

Second Edition

For Sage & Alayna

May you inherit a better world

Chapter 1

Alec had been promising to take me somewhere new for nearly a week, but pack business kept getting in the way. I'd been expecting some posh restaurant in Vegas or maybe LA. The world kind of becomes your oyster when you've got your own jet.

The last thing I'd expected was a picnic up at the top of the mountain that cradled the Graves' estate between large, rocky spurs. It was perfect.

For Alec money was nothing more than a useful tool, but he understood I still wasn't comfortable having that tool used to purchase me things I didn't actually need.

I'd set out determined to hike the whole way up to the top, but I was still a little weak. Apparently everyone had been right about just how much blood I'd lost the night our pack had destroyed the local rival pack. They'd been trying to absorb Alec's pack for the last several years and he hadn't really had any other options, but I knew he still felt uneasy about what had happened.

With his superhuman hearing and sense of smell, Alec knew I was struggling before I even did. He waited though until I finally admitted how tired I was, and then he scooped me up and effortlessly jogged to the top of the peak.

"Are all of you shape shifters such show-offs? At least the change in altitude should bother you a little."

Alec smiled as he came to a stop at the very top and set me down. I waited for a couple of seconds for him to respond and then shrugged and looked out over the arid, Southern Utah landscape.

The view literally took my breath away. I hadn't realized we were quite so close to Zions with all of its incredible greenery. The stark contrast between the desert and the lush vegetation was striking.

"Not a show-off, just really eager to get you up here so I could watch your face when you first saw all of this."

Alec had unzipped his backpack and started emptying it while he spoke. Working with his usual speed, it was only seconds before he had a blanket laid out. He handed me a bottle of water and then helped me down.

"You weren't kidding when you said this place was special."

Alec nodded and then wrapped me in a light blanket. The heat had finally relented slightly. Not enough to actually make it comfortable, but this high up it was actually a little chilly. If I hadn't spent the last several weeks living in the air-conditioned haven of Alec's house, the cooler temperatures at the top of the mountain would have made the trip worthwhile all by themselves.

"I've been wanting to bring you up here for a while. I used to come up here a lot when I was younger. It was kind of an escape after everyone started gaining their wolf form. We were all so closely matched sometimes it seemed like we were always scuffling to establish who was dominant."

He'd sunk down beside me while he was talking, resting with his hands behind his head so he could look up at the few thinly-stretched clouds. I took the opportunity to move closer, cuddling up next to him. I didn't bother looking up at the sky. Truth be told, I had all the beauty I needed right in front of me.

His slight start as my head came to rest on his arm was disappointing but entirely predictable. He adjusted my blanket slightly so it was between us and then pulled me closer. He was perfectly happy to touch me as long as there wasn't any actual skin-on-skin contact. Every time I pushed for more he backed away or found somewhere else he had to be.

"That must have been rough. There are a lot of strong personalities down there."

Alec's chuckle wasn't amused. "You could say that. At first it seemed like things changed up on a daily basis. Then Jasmin manifested her royal wolf form and things settled down a little."

We were venturing into unknown territory for me. Alec was usually so careful to keep me sheltered from his world.

"Was Jasmin dominant then? I mean, if she was a royal wolf and you hadn't manifested your hybrid form yet did she win all of the fights?"

Alec rested his cheek on the top of my head. "Not exactly. If she'd been a little more heartless she probably could have killed me and cowed the rest of the pack. Even then though, it was becoming pretty clear that we couldn't have two separate packs in such close proximity. The need to keep the pack strong meant that even though she pretty much ran the show most of the time there was the occasional thing that I'd just refuse to back down on."

His muscles tightened unconsciously, like maybe he was remembering past pains. "She'd rip me up one side and down the other but on the most important stuff I'd simply out-stubborn her. When the dust settled usually I at least got a compromise we could both live with."

I hugged him tighter for a second. "That sounds a lot like what you guys do right now, just the other way around."

"Yeah. That's about the size of it. She's still hiding something from me, but I'm not willing to bleed her to try and get an answer, not when odds are she'll just refuse to tell me anyways."

That was edging towards a secret that wasn't mine to tell. "Let's talk about something happier."

He looked at me out of the corner of his eye. He'd probably heard my pulse spike. Sometimes the fact that he was a shape shifter instead of just a normal boy was pretty inconvenient. Of course if he wasn't a shape shifter, then he wouldn't be *Alec.*

"Your mom is likely to be back in town pretty soon. Her latest contract has about run its course and it's looking like I'd have to throw a whole bunch of money at her if I wanted to keep her in Europe."

"I'm not so sure that's an improvement in topics."

"You don't want to see your mom?"

"It's not that, it's just that I know we're not going to be able to spend as much time together. It's not like she's going to let me sleep over."

Alec shrugged. "I could try to arrange for her to stay away for another month or two, but with the kind of disposable income she'd get out of the deal it's very possible she'd fly you out there."

"That settles it. Bring her back home. Even the prospect of less time with you is better than being sent out of the country and not seeing you at all."

Alec's smile nearly made me cry. "You know it might be for the best. You need some time to get your bearings again. Going cold turkey is generally the best way to kill an addiction."

We'd been through this more than once since he'd killed Brandon. He'd been so sure he was going to die that he'd relaxed his normally rigid rules. Since then he'd done everything possible to keep me at arm's length. Everything short of sending me away.

Growing up with the example of his mother was a powerful object lesson regarding what happened to humans who got involved with shape shifters; but given enough time, I'd exploit that tiny piece of him that wanted exactly what I wanted.

"Unless you're sending me away there's no point in having this conversation. I'm exactly where I want to be. It's not like I'm throwing myself at you this very second. Have you come up with an explanation for that yet?"

Alec stared back up at the clouds rather than meet my eyes. "Not yet. D...my best guess is maybe that you've realized your best bet at getting what you want long term is to pretend like you're not impacted."

"Please. Do you really believe I have that kind of willpower?"

"After the things I've seen you go through I'd never doubt your willpower, Adri."

It was rare that I suffered from a panic attack in Alec's presence but the reference to what I'd lost, combined with my dreaded nickname, nearly did the trick.

As my pulse sped up again Alec pulled me in close.

"Sorry about that. You do have to admit, it would help explain why you're still here."

"Right, gorgeous, rich boy who also happens to be the next best thing to a superhero. I must be out of my mind not to run for the hills."

"You don't like it when I spend money on you and the more involved you get with me the less likely it is I'll be able to protect you."

"If I let you buy me something will you quit trying to scare me off?"

"No, but it would make me feel better."

He said that last with his heart-stopping blue eyes gazing directly into mine and I nearly stopped breathing. Somehow he hadn't realized yet that when he looked at me like that there wasn't anything I could deny him.

"Okay, you can get me a present, something small and relatively inexpensive."

Alec smiled and reached over to the backpack as he sat up. I let him pull me up and then felt my face freeze as he pulled out a small velvet box.

"Alec, no."

"It wasn't that expensive and you've already told me I could."

"I didn't think you'd have something already ready and waiting to ambush me with. I thought I'd at least have a few days to prepare myself."

He just waited with the box extended and after several seconds I sighed and then gingerly held my hand out. The green velvet lid swung up to reveal the most delicate necklace I'd ever seen. It was a thin glass heart set inside a slightly larger heart.

"I saw it when I was in Virginia last week for business and thought of you."

"It's beautiful. You shouldn't have, but thank you."

Alec slipped it around my neck and did the clasp, his fingers lingering a fraction of an inch from my skin, but he pulled them back without ever actually touching me.

It really was beautiful; I looked back up to thank him again when a wave of weakness slid through me. Alec caught me before I hit the ground.

"Are you okay?"

"I think so. I thought I was past all of this recovery stuff."

He looked concerned but I'd learned to read his expressions better than I think he realized. He was worried, but not just about me. He spent a lot of time worrying. The rest of the pack, the town, his mother, his sister. It was a lot for someone our age to deal with.

"There's an uncommon amount of that going around right now." Alec shook his head at my curious stare. "Dom and Jasmin both seem to be spending more time in bed than you'd expect based on the wounds they took putting down

Cassie and the others. Isaac moved like an old man when we sparred yesterday and Donovan is looking old lately."

I thought back and realized he was right, about Donovan at least. The old shape shifter always moved gingerly thanks to old injuries that had left his right leg permanently crippled. I hadn't thought anything of it at the time but Donovan was looking frailer lately.

The thought of Donovan getting to the point that his age was starting to show nearly made me choke up. I didn't have the extensive history with Donovan that Alec's family had, but he'd been unfailingly kind to me despite the fact that I'd endangered everything he cared about.

Alec correctly read my thoughts. "Don't worry; I'm sure it's nothing. I'll force him to take a couple of days off and I'm sure he'll be fine. He's only a bit past middle age for one of us."

I nearly protested, but Alec was right, it would take an actual order to get Donovan to slow down, and two days was probably pushing it. Donovan somehow managed to respectfully circumvent any order he thought prevented him from taking adequate care of Alec's family.

"Tell me about Christmas at the Paige house."

I blinked a couple of times. The progress I'd made lately notwithstanding, I half expected the question to drive me into a panic attack. Apparently Alec's presence was proof against a second near-attack today.

"I don't know. We always used to do the standard kind of stuff. Presents, eggnog and the Christmas story. Usually Dad made us breakfast Christmas morning and then we'd drive out of the city later in the day and go sledding. I hadn't thought about what it would be like this year."

Alec nodded like he'd just checked a box off on some kind of mental list. "So snow's always been a pretty key ingredient, sounds like."

"I guess. It hadn't sunk in yet that we wouldn't be getting any of that this year. A month ago I would have thought that was a good thing, that it would be one less thing to remind me of Dad and Cindi. I think I might actually miss it this year though."

I rested my head against Alec's shoulder. "It doesn't matter. The important thing now is that we're together for Christmas. Beyond that I don't care what happens."

I was still safely wrapped in my blanket so Alec pulled me into a hug. Even taking into consideration his annoying efforts to protect me from the addictive effect of his touch, this was the happiest I'd ever been. I'd had plenty of bad times over the last year or so to offset the near-perfection of my life now, but it still didn't seem like something that could last.

We just sat there in silence with his arms wrapped around me for several minutes before his cell phone rang. Sometimes I wondered if the slim device was some kind of super spy phone. It seemed to get reception in some of the most incredible places.

He shifted around just enough to answer it without letting go of me with his right arm.

"What's up?"

Whoever was on the other end was talking too quietly for me to make out more than the occasional word.

"...Jack...now...no time..."

I could suddenly feel the energy radiating off of Alec as his beast woke and rose to the surface. His limbs hadn't taken on the fine tremble of someone only seconds away from changing shape, but he was obviously unhappy. Given the tight leash he kept his beast on, I would have been willing to bet that just about anyone else in the pack would have already shifted shapes and ripped a tree out of the ground or done something equally destructive by now.

Alec shifted the phone slightly. I couldn't hear whoever was on the other end anymore, but whatever they'd just said hadn't made things any better. The invisible ants marching up my arms went to double time and the metaphysical breeze that started on his skin and went outward turned into a full-blown gale.

"Stall them. We'll be down in eight minutes. If worse comes to worst, you two contain Isaac and tell Dom to sit on Jack. Keep Rachel out of the way."

Already moving with the unearthly speed he normally concealed even from me, Alec hung up the phone and started throwing things into the backpack.

"Jack's working himself up to a dominance fight with Jess. This couldn't have happened at a worse time. If we're not back before it starts odds are someone's going to die."

Chapter 2

I tried to convince Alec to leave me behind. He could run much faster without me, but we'd never managed to track Vincent down. It was a remote risk, but Alec spent the odd moment worrying about whether or not Vincent was lurking in the area hoping for a chance to get back at us.

I was still arguing when he put the backpack on me, picked me up, and started running. He'd swung me around behind him by the second step and then there was nothing left to do but hold on.

I tried closing my eyes but the first time he dropped down a cliff it was all I could do not to scream and I quickly decided it was better to see what was coming than be taken completely by surprise.

Alec wasn't just fast, he was incredibly agile too. If I'd doubted his ability to get us to the bottom of the mountain in less than ten minutes the doubt vanished in the first thirty seconds of the adrenaline-filled dash.

We jumped a respectable-sized ravine and then leaped out into empty air, skipping from one branch to another and then sliding down the bare trunk of a dying pine tree. It wasn't a smooth descent. I suspected that Alec left blood and skin on the bark before we hit the ground.

Only his well-muscled arm stretched back around me kept me from being jarred off of his back. The gravity-fueled first part of our run was bad enough but once we got to more level ground Alec put on a burst of speed that turned trees and rocks into barely-seen blurs that were past almost before I registered their presence. Alec running flat out on a level road was one thing; in the forest it was simply terrifying.

Only the thought of one of my friends bleeding and dying kept me from begging Alec to stop. I was surprised when Alec veered towards the training ground rather than continuing on to the house.

I had a heartbeat to hope that Alec's sister Rachel, a normal human like me, was safely home and then we slid to a halt on the hot sand.

The whole pack was there, and I immediately understood why most of them had changed shapes. The energy in the air tore at me like a chorus of buzz saws; the united pack that had recently faced down Brandon's larger group of thugs looked like it was only seconds away from turning on itself.

It was Jess who was in the center of the circle, faced off against Jack. I felt my throat tighten up. Jess and I weren't exactly friends but I was pretty sure she hadn't done anything to deserve having Jack tear into her. Jack was one of the new wolves Alec had absorbed into the pack when he'd killed Brandon. Apparently three of the rival pack hadn't ever been quite as bad, so when they came to us and requested protection, Alec hadn't had the heart to turn them away.

Sometimes I wished he had. At least Jack—he was always in everyone's face, and I had a suspicion that he wasn't going to be fighting fair. He'd spent his formative years in such a brutal environment it was almost inevitable that he'd do something dirty. He didn't fight just to win, he fought to intimidate so that nobody else would be willing to face off against him.

Dom and the other submissives were milling around the outside of the circle while James and Jasmin were obviously trying to keep Isaac from interfering. I opened my mouth, maybe to ask everyone to calm down, and Jack sprang at Jess.

Scraps of cloth went flying as both fighters shifted and clinched. Their coloration was too similar. For a second it looked like Jess was on top and then the pair shifted around again and I lost track of who was who.

Big splashes of crimson stained the sand now and the growls were interspersed with whines of pain. The rest of the pack wasn't hindered by my merely human eyes. I watched them out of a corner of my eye for some clue of who was winning.

Isaac crouched forward as a particularly loud yelp signaled trouble for Jess. On the other side of the circle Alison had shrunk down on all four paws. Jack had been her friend for years but she mostly just seemed like she wanted the fighting to stop.

The whirling bundle of fangs and blood wasn't moving as quickly now. It looked like Jack was on top now, his fangs fastened on Jess's throat. She unsuccessfully tried to shake him off and then stopped moving with a final whine.

Isaac knocked James and Jasmin back and crossed over to Jack, ripping him off of Jess. The movements were so fast I had to intuit them based off of their effects. The rest of the pack seemed to spring into action at the same time. There was a flurry of motion, but the only thing I registered was Isaac following Jack's flying form, intent on finishing the smaller wolf.

Alec had been standing next to me, but somehow he arrived at Jack first. Alec's hulking hybrid form knocked Isaac to one side and then spun around just in time to catch Jack mid-spring. James arrived a split second later to help restrain Isaac. I'd expected to see Jasmin accompanying him, but she'd joined Dom in facing down Sam and Alison, who looked like they wanted to help their friend.

Jack was thrashing in Alec's grip now, and Isaac had turned on James with a killing fury. Even I could see there wasn't time for Alec to be gentle, not with the growing pool of blood around Jess. Alec threw Jack up against a tree and then turned and tackled Isaac.

"You're stopping us from helping Jess!"

The words came out deep and harsh from Alec's shifted throat, but they got through to Isaac. He stopped struggling instantly and James and Alec rolled off him a few seconds later. I half expected Jack to rush Isaac again. Instead as Isaac melted back down into his normal human form, Jack limped over to Alec and dropped down so his belly was in the sand.

Dom had already shifted back and was applying pressure to the worst of Jess' injuries. Alec took in Jess' wounds and then turned back to Jack. "Stay out of Isaac's way."

Alec waved James and Jasmin after Isaac and Dom and then hurried back to me. "I've got to go with them. James will need help if...well, if things go badly. It's not safe for you back at the house right now. Are you okay here for half an hour or so? Then you can have Alison bring you back."

My mind shied away from the implications of what he'd just avoided saying. Jess dead, Isaac losing control and having to be restrained. Alec was right. There were too many people back at the house already who couldn't protect themselves. Rachel, Donovan, Alec's mom. Plus James' mom and Jess' dad.

Alison's welcoming presence notwithstanding, I probably would have just headed back up the mountain by myself so as to avoid being around Jack. Alec was right though. If Vincent really hadn't cleared out of the area I'd be much safer with Alison and Sam around than off by myself.

Alec waited for my nod of acceptance and then turned back to Jack and the others. "If anything happens to Adri that you could have stopped, I'll hunt you all down."

It could have been an idle threat, but the words were accompanied by a flash of power. I'd never felt anything like it before, but it sounded like Alec had just bound both him and his beast. If they let me get hurt, then his beast would essentially take over and run the three of them to the ground. It wasn't a thing to do lightly but it was exactly the kind of thing I'd come to expect out of Alec. He always did his absolute best to take care of those who depended on him.

As soon as the three submissive wolves nodded understanding, Alec took off in a blur. The fact that he was moving so quickly and didn't bother changing back to his human form was a testament to just how badly he was needed back at the house.

As Jack melted back into his normal form Alison and Sam hurried over to his side.

"Stay back a little please, Adri. Until we know for sure how bad his injuries are, he isn't safe."

Alison's pleasant alto voice was distorted slightly with worry, worry for Jack, worry for me, worry for herself if something happened to me.

Sam looked up just enough to confirm that I was keeping my distance and then nodded. "She's right. When one of us is injured past a certain point our beasts can sometimes take over. It doesn't happen often, but when it does the injured wolf goes berserk."

Alison used a length of cloth off of her discarded shirt to stem some of the bleeding, placing Sam's hands on the area to apply pressure before she moved on to the next injury while he continued explaining.

"If there's a powerful, dominant hybrid around they can compel the injured beast into submission, but if there isn't, your best bet is to just beat on the injured wolf until it collapses into a coma and then try and keep it alive once it's not trying to rip your head off."

I was pretty sure Alec wouldn't have been overjoyed to know that his newest wolves were letting so much slip, but I wasn't about to tell him. I'd spent entirely too much time wishing I knew exactly this kind of stuff. He claimed my ignorance would help protect me but I was less and less convinced he was right the more I found out about his world.

I shifted around so I could see Jack's face. He looked unconscious, which probably meant he was safe, at least until he woke up, but I didn't get any closer.

"What happened? I mean I know dominance challenges are kind of a fact of life in a shape shifter pack, but this seemed crazy. I mean I don't think I've ever seen Isaac lose his cool like that."

Sam looked at Alison for a second and I was momentarily struck by just how odd their pairing was. She was one of the kindest people I knew. I mean like Rachel or Dominic kind. He was much more edgy, not Jack or James edgy, but edgy enough I wouldn't have expected him to fall in love with Alison or for her to return the sentiment. Then again, it seemed like everyone in the pack had some kind of odd love interest. James and Dom, Isaac and Jess. Heck, when you got right down to it, those were normal compared to the thought of rich, gorgeous, perfect Alec liking me.

Sam cleared his throat uncomfortably. "Actually, I think that was my fault. I was trying to calm Jack down, you know how he gets. Anyways I was trying to point out the stupidity of going after Jess when she was with Isaac. It sort of came out wrong and I think I pissed him off."

Things had been pretty tense before. The night Alec had rescued me from two of Brandon's wolves, Jasmin, Jess and James had nearly staged a coup d'état. Still there had always been the sense that the bonds the pack had forged while standing up to Brandon's pack were ultimately too strong to allow that kind of catastrophe to take place.

I was starting to wonder though how much of the unity had been shared closeness and how much of it had simply been an understanding that they had to all hang together or Brandon would hang them individually.

"I always thought things would get better after we beat Brandon. I never imagined that they could actually get worse. At least we helped get the three of you out from under his thumb. Every day must have been terrifying with him, Cassie and Vincent around."

Sam shrugged but didn't look up from Jack's still-bleeding form. "It's all about the same. The life of a submissive pretty much sucks wherever you are. At least there we..."

I saw Alison look up out of the corner of my eye, the movement inhumanly fast, an expression that almost looked like terror on her face before it settled into the expressionless mask I was realizing all of the submissives developed.

"Sam!"

"Sorry." He looked up at me as he said it, leaving me with the impression he hadn't been sorry, that there was more he'd have told me if Alison wasn't there.

It was one of the more disturbing conversations I'd had recently. I'd been through more with Alec's pack in the last couple of months than I like to think about. They'd primarily been backing up Alec, but by doing so they'd also supported me when it would have been easier to give me to Brandon and just hope for the best.

I didn't really like all of them, but I'd thought I could trust them. If someone was going around abusing the three new members of the pack then they weren't the person I'd thought they were.

Chapter 3

I was sleeping alone these days. Not that Alec and I had ever done anything more than just sleep. Frankly I was still a little freaked out about the idea of crossing that line. Most girls my age seemed to do that kind of stuff without a second thought, but it wasn't something I was eager to jump into. Still, I really did miss waking up next to Alec every morning.

Alison and Sam had stabilized Jack and then we'd headed back to the house. The three of them actually lived in one of the smaller dwellings scattered around the grounds, but Alison had been uncharacteristically firm and demanded that I let her accompany me all the way to my room.

It'd been looking like she was going to camp out on my floor until Alec showed back up to release her from the assignment to protect me. Luckily Rachel had shown up and shooed her off. A normal human like me, Rachel shouldn't have really had any standing in the pack. If it wasn't for the fact that Alec had invested her with a hefty chunk of his authority as alpha, she would have been a second-class citizen.

From what little bit I'd been able to tease out of the various members of the pack it was an unheard of measure for an alpha to take. It was a sign of both just how much Alec trusted her and how much he loved her. Not every brother would put himself that much in harm's way just to make his sister's life a little more bearable.

When Rachel had told Alison that she'd accept responsibility with Alec if something happened to me, it was enough to reassure Alison she could leave.

Rachel hadn't had much in the way of news. Apparently Jess's wounds were a lot worse even than I'd realized, and the rest of the pack was busy dealing with the fallout.

I'd thought about calling Alec for an update. I'd really wanted to hear his voice at least, but given the fact that he had been forced to shift without stripping down to the stretchy ha'bit they all wore, his phone was probably still up at the training ground. I should have thought to grab it before I left.

Rachel had tried to reassure me that everything would be okay, but she was too worn around the edges for it to be very believable. The tip-toeing, waiting-for-the-other-shoe-to-drop feeling hadn't just been impacting the shape shifters. It didn't help that she seemed to have caught some kind of bug. Nothing serious, just enough to deplete her energy levels.

It was actually a relief when she finally left. Pretending that we weren't worried, that everything was bound to be okay was surprisingly exhausting. I'd nibbled on some of the dry food Alec had packed for the picnic, finished up some of the homework I'd been procrastinating and then finally turned in a good three hours early.

With a solid night's sleep behind me, lonely though it had been, I felt quite a bit better. I hurried through my morning routine and sighed in relief when I found Alec waiting for me at the breakfast table.

He poured me a bowl of my favorite cold cereal and a tall glass of orange juice and then held my chair as I sat down. He'd been on a real 'Adri needs to eat' kick ever since I'd been injured.

"Is Jess going to be okay?"

"It looks that way. We'll have to keep her home for a day or two to avoid all kinds of questions at school, but she seems stable. Past the point of us having to worry she's going to lose control and attack Dom or Donovan."

I nodded in relief and then started in on my cereal. Alec would either tell me more or not. I'd pretty much learned that there was no point pestering him for more information.

"It's going to play havoc with everyone's schedule though. Isaac was scheduled for a couple of business trips over the next little bit. We're trying to sweep up as much of Brandon's financial empire as we can before the vultures start circling. A lot of his factors aren't particularly trustworthy. Once they stop getting instructions from the top we can probably convince them to sell off pieces at huge discounts. He's always relied mostly on fear to keep his people in line."

The sudden concern with cash was the last thing I'd expected out of Alec. "I thought we, I mean you, were pretty much set for life."

Alec nodded. "Donovan's got more assets under management than any eight people could conceivably spend in a lifetime as long as they exercised a modicum of restraint. It's not about that though. Half of the reason we were able to hold Brandon off as long as we did was the fact that we had considerably more economic clout than he did."

Alec finished peeling his orange and shrugged. "Standing off a more powerful opponent is all about making them understand that although they could kill you, they'd get hurt too badly in the process to make it worthwhile. If we can't do that physically, there's always the chance we can do it economically."

"So we're not really out of the woods yet then?"

"I'm afraid not."

After news like that I really didn't want to eat. We'd barely scraped through our last near-death situation, and we'd been a relatively tight-knit group then. How could we possibly survive another if we were eating at each other like this?

"I got confirmation last night. Your mom will be flying back into town soon."

"Great. It's like knowing I've got to go back to prison."

Alec's expression solidified into the mask he'd always used when dealing with Brandon. "Actually I think it would be a good idea for you to go home today after school. Given how things have been recently it would be safer for you there."

It was like being dunked in ice water. He continued on while I was still trying to come up with the right protest.

"Donovan had your house cleaned last week so you won't need to worry about that, but it'd probably be best if you were there for a couple of days to give it a more lived-in feel. I know that Rachel will want to spend some time over there if you'll have her. She's been chomping at the bit to exercise some of the freedom available her now that the threat of Brandon's pack isn't continually hanging over us."

I nodded, not because I was convinced, but because I knew fighting with him over something like this wasn't the way to go. Whoever had said that bit about picking your battles had probably been thinking of Alec when they'd said it.

"Will you come over too? Maybe stay the night?"

A trace of longing flashed across his face before the mask mostly settled back into place. "I'm not sure that's a good idea. Things are still too unsettled around here. I'd thought maybe they were cooling down a bit, but you saw what happened when we left on that picnic."

It was probably even true, but it wasn't the only reason. He was still fixated on that Ja'tell bond, still trying to do what he thought was the right thing.

The drive into school was more subdued than normal. Rachel even forwent her usual plea for Alec to put a better stereo system in her car. When our motorcade rolled into school it was to more of the furtive looks and hushed conversations I'd come to expect.

I kept telling myself that nobody our age was going to be able to keep the disappearance of nearly all of Brandon's pack at the forefront of their minds forever. It was hard to believe that with the police in the school every day though.

I'd been pulled in for questioning twice already. I'd stuck to the story Alec had outlined. We'd all been together roasting marshmallows around a campfire to finish out our Ashure Day celebration. I hated lying to the cops, to anyone really, but the police especially. Alec was right though, it wasn't like we could tell them the truth. Nobody would ever believe that Brandon had been an evil shape shifter out to kill Alec and enslave the rest of us.

The well-known rivalry between Alec and Brandon made us immediate suspects. If not for the fact that apparently the local judge and chief of police both owed Alec some pretty huge favors things probably would have gotten worse.

I'd expected Alison, Sam and Jack being with us to take some of the pressure off, but so far it hadn't helped. Still, Jasmin was right. As long as we all stuck to the same story eventually the police would have to close the case. Alec apparently had a whole team of very high-powered lawyers on his payroll and they'd already started making noises about police harassment.

Some of the pack members had swapped their classes around now that Rachel and I didn't need constant babysitting, but I still shared Biology with Alec. Mrs. Sorenson had seriously mellowed out in the last few weeks, so as long as we kept it down we pretty much had carte blanche.

Normally Alec used the time to tease more details out of me regarding my life before Sanctuary. He was just as attentive as ever, but I could tell there was something bothering him.

My mom coming back? The escalating tension among the rest of the pack? I discarded a dozen different ideas on how to pull him out of his shell, and then class was over.

Alec gingerly hugged me, no skin on skin contact, as he dropped me off at English and then it was time to face Britney again. Actually it was all much less dramatic than that, but outside of the pack, Britney was my biggest concern.

She'd taken Brandon's disappearance incredibly hard. Not only had she liked him, apparently he or one of his pack had let slip that they were headed over to kick the crap out of us. Given the way her father had been poking at some of the inevitable anomalies that had surfaced lately, it seemed only a matter of time before he started believing her. Her history of lying to manipulate him had so far been working against her, but she showed no sign of backing down over her claims that Alec's friends had to be involved in Brandon's disappearance, and the uncharacteristic determination was bound to eventually convince him. He wasn't in law enforcement or anything, but he was pretty well-respected. So if he really started pushing, it was bound to cause more problems.

"Killed anyone lately, Adri?"

"I don't know what you're talking about."

I should have just ignored her.

"Eventually the cops are going to come up with evidence that Alec won't be able to suppress.

When they do I'll be first in line to testify against you. Brandon was twice the man Alec is."

"Look, Britney, I'm sorry that we had that falling out. I'm sorry that you're all alone now, but you need to understand that Brandon never loved you. He never even really liked you. He was using you, and whatever might have happened to send him away doesn't matter. What really matters is that you've got another chance to do something with your life instead of just sitting here and pining after him."

It was a long shot. I had no real way to know for sure she was addicted to him, but Alec wouldn't have gone on and on about the Ja'tell bond if it hadn't been real, hadn't been dangerous. Not every human who got entangled with a shape shifter was going to end up like his mom, but none of us really came away completely unscathed.

Britney stared at me for a moment and then the hate melted away into something else. It was like she was five again and I'd just taken away her brand new kitten.

"I'm not pining. I'll have you know I've started dating a guy from Reno. He's varsity football and his parents are as rich as Alec's mom."

The words were too practiced. She wrapped her arms around herself even as she said them.

I opened my mouth to respond but she opened her book and turned away from me.

I spent the rest of the class pretending to read The Count of Monte Cristo. It was actually a pretty interesting story so far, but my mind was too full of thoughts of Alec and Britney, strife and Ja'tell bonds.

When the bell finally released us, it was a relief to go to Algebra. Mrs. Campbell ran us through a new concept in record time and then released us to work on our assignment. Jasmin hadn't ever changed out of the class after Brandon's pack had been eliminated. We still weren't as close as Rachel and I, or even Dom and I, but it'd been a definite peace offering.

When one of the aides brought a note from the office and Mrs. Campbell left, Jasmin scooted her desk right over so we could whisper.

"Was that a crazy fight last night or what?"

"I guess. I mean I still don't really know what's normal."

Jasmin seemed to consider what she could get away with telling me and then shrugged. "It varies from pack to pack, but Jack must have a death wish or something. Isaac could rip him in half without breaking a sweat. Once we got back to the house, Alec had to all but sit on Isaac to keep Jack and Sam both alive for another day."

"Things were still tense after the fight then?"

"Yeah. Alec and James forced Isaac out of the house to keep him out of Donovan's way. Then while Donovan was trying to sew Jess up, her dad showed up."

"Oh, poor Andrew."

I'd always liked Jess' dad. I hadn't had much to do with him, but every time our paths had crossed he'd been the epitome of good breeding.

Jasmin snorted. "Poor Andrew nothing. It's us you should be feeling sorry for. He completely freaked out."

Confined as Andrew was to the wheelchair that provided his only source of mobility, it seemed hard to believe he'd been able to cause Jasmin much in the way of problems. Some of my disbelief must have shown through.

"He's all messed up from what Agony did to him, but if he's angry enough not to notice the pain when the scar tissue pulls, he's still dangerous. He took one look at Jess bleeding away on the operating table and shifted. I barely had time to knock him out of the way. I tried to back him down with a display of power, but I'm not in Alec's class so it got ugly."

That last sentence had just the barest trace of resentment. Jasmin hated not having control of her destiny, hated that she had to take second place not just to Alec but also occasionally to Isaac and James too.

I waited expectantly. I could generally draw more information out of Jasmin if I was patient. It was probably another form of peace offering.

"You have no idea how hard it is to restrain someone when we're...furry. I had to just grab a hold of his neck and hope I could hold on tight enough to control him without going too far and killing him."

The picture of Andrew lying on the floor bleeding while his daughter was doing the same above him on the table sent chills through me.

"Everyone's okay now though?"

"More or less. Jess is going to make a full recovery and Dom got Alec to us pretty quickly. Alec was able to force Andrew back down into his normal shape. Good thing too. When Donovan checked the old man he found all kinds of internal bleeding. Apparently the scar tissue pulls on his organs when he gets out of control like that. He could actually bleed himself out internally if he kept ignoring the pain."

It all fit with the kind of craziness I'd seen out of the pack before, but it just didn't make sense. "Why would he attack you guys when you were busy helping save Jess? It doesn't make any sense!"

Jasmin shrugged again. "You have to remember that our beasts don't think the way you and I do. To us it's ludicrous, but it's the same kind of thing that made Isaac attack James while Alec was helping calm Andrew down. By the time all was said and done last night everyone but Dom and Donovan were bleeding."

Jasmin slid her desk back to its normal place a split second before Mrs. Campbell came back through the door.

If there was one teacher you couldn't get away with talking during their class, it was her. I was halfway through another problem when Jasmin passed me her cellphone. There was a text from Alec on the screen.

Please let Adri know her mom is on a flight back to the U.S. She'll be home tomorrow.

Chapter 4

Isaac had left Mom's flight information when he came over that night to disconnect the nifty equipment that forwarded our land line to the cellphone Alec had given me. I tried to get Isaac to take the phone with him but he'd politely refused.

I'd made a mental note to keep the stupid thing hidden, finished up my homework, and gone to bed.

School the next day had been depressingly lonely. Rachel was the only member of the pack who hadn't skipped school and I didn't have any classes with her. We'd visited a little during lunch but with all of the people around I couldn't ask her any of the questions I really wanted to know.

She'd told me that everyone was okay, and moved on to the kind of meaningless small talk neither of us really enjoyed.

After lunch, I'd absently gone from class to class with my stomach getting steadily more and more queasy. I'd never really kept this kind of big secret from my mom, and I was a terrible liar. Under normal circumstances that would be bad enough, but if I couldn't keep her ignorant of everything that had happened over the last few weeks then I'd lose even what little bit of access I'd otherwise have to Alec.

I knew for a fact Alec loved me, but given the way he was closing me out, I was more than slightly worried that he'd talk himself into deciding that I'd be better off without him.

By the time school finally ended and I met up with Rachel in front of her yellow VW Bug, I was pretty subdued.

"Adri, it's not the end of the world, it's just your mom."

"Right, except that it's going to mean I'm even more disconnected from the pack. I've only been gone for two days and I'm already completely out of the loop."

"Yeah. Well, you're really not missing out on that much, just more posturing and dominance games."

"Is Alec okay?"

"Yeah, he's had something on his mind for a couple of days now, but I'm sure it will blow over soon. Alec's spent so many years freaking out about Brandon's pack it's like a reflex now.

He probably feels odd if he's not worried about something."

"I guess. I just wish he'd talk to me. I feel like it's been forever since we just talked."

Rachel shrugged as she zipped around another curve. "Don't let it bother you too much; he really is crazy about you. Speaking of people being crazy about people, did Jasmin talk to you about Ben yesterday?"

"No. The only time we were alone together was Algebra and we only had a couple of minutes while Mrs. Campbell was gone."

"What a coward. She's still busted up about having to leave the dance before he showed up. If he showed up. He's been avoiding her again, which probably means he's back to using."

"Wait, Ben's an addict?"

"Whoops, I thought you knew. Don't judge him too harshly. He's had a rougher life than just about anyone else you'll ever meet. Abusive dad, suicidal mom, crap relatives, you name it."

I nodded. Maybe a year ago I would have been all snotty and said it shouldn't matter where you came from, you should still be able to stay clean, but lately I was a lot more conscious of just how little it could take to bring someone's world crashing down on them. I still mostly figured that kind of stuff was a choice, but it was hard to throw stones considering how much a wreck I'd been less than a month ago, and how far I still had to go.

"He's a good guy. He hates the crap but always falls back into it eventually." Rachel looked away from the road just long enough to make sure I was paying attention and then shrugged. "Anyways, you need to meet him so you can see for yourself. Not only that, I think Jasmin could use some help convincing him that she's for real."

"Really, she's told him she likes him and he's not falling all over her?"

"Not in so many words, but near enough. Like I said, he's had a rough life. He's not the most trusting guy you'll ever meet."

It was intriguing. I'd had a hard time believing it when Brandon had told me Ben wasn't interested in Jasmin. Once I realized what a jerk Brandon was I'd just kind of assumed he'd lied to me about that too. The concept of any guy not wanting gorgeous, perfect Jasmin strained the limits of reality.

"Okay, I'll keep an eye out for an opportunity to talk to him, but don't hold your breath. These days nobody besides you guys talks to me."

"I guess. I just had a feeling like you needed to be in the loop. Since Jasmin was too bashful to do it yesterday."

Her voice had taken on an odd tone, one that sounded strangely familiar. We pulled onto my dusty lane and I felt my heart race when I saw the Jeep parked on the concrete pad. Rachel pulled up behind Mom's car and shifted into park while I was still trying to decide where I'd heard that tone before.

Mom raced out of the house a split second later, opening the passenger's side door and hugging me before I'd even managed to get my seatbelt off.

"Adriana! I kept telling myself that you still had an hour and a half of tutoring left but I was just about ready to come get you anyways."

"Hi, Mom. This is my friend Rachel."

Mom and Rachel really hit it off. It was probably just because Mom was relieved that I had an actual, honest-to-goodness friend. They exchanged small talk about Mom's trip and the weather and then Rachel excused herself to go home and finish up some schoolwork.

I followed Mom into the house and helped make dinner while she told me all about the trip to Italy for the original job. They'd been shooting in a little town south of Rome that still had narrow, cobblestone streets. The way she described the restaurants, people and hills almost made me jealous.

As we finished eating, Mom's stories finally wound down. She described the last of the 'miracle' jobs that arrived in succession as each prior engagement came to an end, and then shrugged.

"So that about sums it up. What's been going on here while I've been gone?"

"The same old stuff. School, homework and more school."

"Come on, sweetie. You had to have done something besides that. What about that boy you liked? Brandon, was it?"

I'd spent the occasional hour or so since Alec had told me Mom was coming back wondering if she'd even remember that Brandon and I had broken up.

"He...he was a lot like you warned me he would be. When I wouldn't do the things he wanted, he broke up with me."

Mom leaned over and wrapped her arms around me. "Oh, sweetie. Are you...I mean did he hurt you?"

"No, I'm fine. He's old news."

"Are you sure?"

I mustered up a convincing smile. "I'm fine, really. He's ancient history, which is more than I can say for my homework, which is unfortunately due all too soon."

"Okay, Adri. You go up and work on that and I'll clean up down here."

I headed upstairs and even managed to keep my tears under control until I made it safely to my room.

It was stupid to cry and I knew it, but I couldn't stop myself. The kegger had happened weeks ago and Brandon hadn't even done anything to me. I didn't know if that was even it. It was more reasonable to think I was crying over the fact that Alec was keeping me at arm's length. I was tired of being so alone. Ever since Cindi and Dad had died I'd had no one.

I heard Mom coming up the stairs and pulled myself together enough to wish her good night and then it was just me.

I cried into my pillow for a little while before remembering the phone Alec had given me. Trembling fingers input a text.

I missed you today.

It felt like such a lame thing to say, simultaneously too revealing and not enough. I only had to wait a second before my phone vibrated in response.

I missed you too. What are you doing?

Wishing I could talk to you.

That's good news. Check your window.

I ran to the window and felt a smile break out when I saw Alec, in hybrid form, climbing up our light pole. He carefully reached over, sank his claws into the roof and then swung into my room. He shifted back so smoothly that his bare feet landed on my floor rather than the wicked talons that would have otherwise ruined my hardwood floor.

I wrapped my arms around Alec before he could evade me.

"It's so good to see you."

He rested his cheek on the top of my head and sighed. "It's good to see you again too. Would you think I was incredibly pathetic if I told you I'd headed over this way half an hour ago in the hopes that your mom's light would go out before yours did? I've been kind of worried that having her back would be a tough adjustment for you."

"No, I don't think it's pathetic. I think that's the most thoughtful thing anyone's done for me in a while."

Carefully holding me by the shoulders, Alec stepped back far enough that he could see the evidence of my crying jag. He had to have known as soon as he arrived. He'd probably been hoping if he gave me a few seconds to adjust that we could talk about it without me falling completely apart.

"Are you okay? I knew it would be hard to go back to living by your mom's rules but I didn't think there'd be tears involved."

The words and tone were both perfect. A double helping of concern and a touch of humor intended to defuse any awkwardness.

I hid my head against his chest as fresh tears broke free of my eyes. It was all I could do to mute the sobs but I had to. If Mom came in right now she'd freak out.

Alec picked me up and carried me over to my bed. Moving like I weighed nothing at all, he wrapped me in a sheet and then curled up next to me.

"It's okay. You're not alone anymore. You have the whole pack and I'll do everything I can to keep you safe."

It would have been the perfect opportunity to tell him exactly what was bothering me, but there wasn't anything he could do about it. He wasn't lying. He'd do everything he was able to protect me, to love me, but there was no guarantee it would be enough. More and more I was understanding that there were far too many things out of his control. He was bigger than life, bigger than me, and it felt like only a matter of time before he was pulled away from me despite all either of us could do.

In the end, I chose silence and he gently rocked me until I fell asleep.

Chapter 5

It was crazy, but after everything that had happened to me over the last few weeks, I'd almost expected Mom's trip to have changed her. I'd thought maybe I'd wake up to a home-cooked breakfast like Dad used to make. Instead the usual note had been waiting for me on the kitchen white board.

Gone to shoot a promising location I saw while prepping the pamphlet. I'll be home before you're back from tutoring. Love you.

—Mom

I still hadn't told Mom I'd quit the tutoring lab. It wasn't the kind of news designed to make a parent feel like everything was going the way it ought to be. I pushed the thought aside, grabbed a packet of string cheese to nibble on and headed outside.

Alec was waiting in my driveway, and his smile lit up my face in return.

"I thought maybe I'd have to catch the school bus."

"I've been thinking about you since I had to leave this morning. I was hoping that your mom would leave early today so I could drive you in to town."

Alec helped me into his car and then we were rolling down the lane.

"Alec...thank you. For last night I mean. I don't mean to be one of those needy, whiny girls. It's just..."

He turned the full force of his gaze on me and it was like my brain hiccupped. "You don't have to worry about anything. It's I who should be thanking you. I needed last night as much or more than you did. Thank you, Adriana Paige, for being who you are."

Now that I was caught up with the rest of the class in Algebra, life was easier, scholastically speaking. During biology Alec and I listened with one ear while we played a game of 'Would You Rather.'

Alec kept throwing curve balls in the game and somehow I ended up stuck in the Swiss Alps with a snowboard that was missing the back bindings and a price on my head.

Alec walked me to my next class and then time stuttered by until lunch. Rachel met Jasmin and me at our lockers.

"Alec asked me to let the two of you know he's not going to be around for lunch. He said he's sorry, but I think it's the perfect opportunity for us to have some quality girl talk."

Jasmin actually blushed and then the rest of the pack arrived and it was too late. As we grabbed our food and sat at our normal table I counted heads and realized we were down more than just Alec.

"Where's Sam?"

Alison shrugged. "With Alec. They didn't say what they were up to, just that they were going to be gone for an hour or so."

The conversation between the girls skittered around for a minute or two before Rachel got everyone busy talking about another shopping trip to Vegas. Everyone made a valiant effort to include me, but I just couldn't lose myself in the idea of buying more pretty clothes that I'd never be able to wear for fear my mom would freak out. She was plenty self-absorbed most of the time, but if I came back sporting the kind of clothes Rachel was going to want to buy me, she'd instantly know I'd spent more money than I could possibly have made in two years of working at the tutor lab.

The boys were discussing motorcycles. As usual when it came to boisterous conversation, James had taken the lead.

"I'm telling you, man. The new 900cc Kawasaki has way more potential than the other bikes this year. You could easily crank another twenty horses out of that thing without even replacing any hardware."

Isaac shook his head. "I don't know. I mean you're right that the Kawasaki is a better machine but those things are already pushed pretty close to spec. I'm not sure even you can crank that kind of power just by tweaking the fuel map."

James shook his head in mock disbelief. "You're crazy, man. They aren't cars, but it's the same principle."

Jack chuckled along with Isaac. "You're both wrong. I happen to know on good authority that Alec just ordered another R1. Now that's a machine. It starts out with ten percent more power and it's got a frame that's fifteen percent lighter."

It was like a cold front had just blown in. Isaac turned towards Jack and suddenly the air was dancing with invisible shape shifter energy. An answering flare of power rushed out from Jack but it was obvious he was outclassed.

Jack still didn't look like he was going to back down though until James turned on him as well. The other members of the pack were all buzzing with power too, but it was just the reflex response to danger, not the hostile presence the two hybrids were generating.

Alison reached out to Jack, possibly just to try and calm him down, but I noticed Jasmin go utterly still at the motion. Jas wasn't paying attention to Jack, but she was ready to take

Alison down if things boiled over to some kind of confrontation.

For a brief moment things teetered on the edge of violence and then Jack looked down and the tension slowly melted away. It was the kind of freaky thing that had happened all the time when Brandon had been trying to drive us into a misstep, but it felt wrong to happen when we were all supposed to be on the same side.

The group broke up before lunch was over, all heading off in separate directions in an attempt to regain our composure before we had to interact with the humans again. I felt myself rubbing my arms. Apparently it had been too long since I'd seen the preliminaries when shape shifters were about to throw down. It hadn't affected me this badly before.

Mrs. Campbell stopped me near my locker.

"Adriana, I've been meaning to talk to you. The load at the tutoring lab has gone up over the last two weeks. I don't know if you're still unavailable, but I'd love to have you back."

I felt a surge of relief as she offered me a way out of the looming confrontation with my mom.

"That would be really great, Mrs. Campbell. Things have really opened up lately for me and I'd love to help out."

"Well then, shall we say tonight? I'll let Albert know to expect you."

I all but skipped to my locker and opened it. I never expected to find a note sitting on top of my physics book. For a heartbeat I thought maybe it was from Alec, but I opened it to find Sam's awkward scrawl.

Alec wanted me to let you know he's going to be out for the rest of the day. Alison wants me to see if you want to do lunch Saturday, and I wanted to let you know that I'm getting writer's cramp.

—Sam

By the time school ended I was definitely missing Alec. It was going to take a lot more effort than I'd realized to re-accustom myself to only seeing him an hour or two per day. I was trying to distract myself by working on homework when Albert stopped by my table.

"Hey now, we don't hold with any of that history stuff here."

Albert had always been able to draw a smile out of me.

"Some of us have better things to do than just sitting around solving equations all day."

"Ouch." Albert sat down on the edge of the table. "So how have you been? We've missed you around here."

"I'm okay. Just been a lot of things going on lately. What about you? How's Fatal Angst?"

I could always count on steering the conversation around to his band to make Albert uncomfortable.

"They're not bad. We got a new bassist who also does backup vocals. Some of the guys are starting to talk big."

His tone was casual, but something he really didn't care about wouldn't have made him so uncomfortable. I guess it's possible to get desensitized to that feeling, but mostly it seemed like the strongest reactions are all driven by how important something is to us. I wasn't going to 'out' him though.

"That's great. I mean I hope you guys go really far."

Albert rolled his eyes. "Right, we'll be topping the charts next week. It's nice though, the sound's starting to come together. Hey, you should come down and take in a set sometime."

That was dangerous. Not for me, not really. Skin addiction or not, I was starting to really understand that my heart would always belong to Alec. It was dangerous for Albert though.

"Thanks, but now that my mom's back in town I'm lucky to make it ten minutes away to visit Alec. I'm pretty sure she'd freak out if I said I wanted to go to Vegas to take in a real-live rock group."

He flinched a little but mustered up a smile as he said his good byes.

I more or less sleepwalked through helping the few students who hung around until my shift, and then came up for air when Rachel bounced over and hugged me.

"Hey, Dom texted me for help. Don't worry though, I arranged you a perfectly good ride."

I followed her gesture, half expecting to find one of the jocks we both detested. Alec's smile as my eyes found him sent butterflies rampaging about my stomach.

"Sorry I missed class again. Can I make it up to you on the way home?"

The drive home was companionable. There was plenty of silence, but it wasn't the kind of quiet that awkwardly demanded I try and drown it out.

"So I've got some good news for you and some bad, Miss Paige."

"You're not starting off great if you're still hoping to make up for ditching out on me again."

Alec chuckled at my attempted humor. "The bad news is I'm going out of town for a few days. A week tops."

My mood imploded. "Where now?"

He always got the same look when he was trying to tiptoe past something he didn't think it was safe for me to know.

"I don't think I can tell you that, not right now. Suffice it to say it's work-related and it's not a trip I'd be taking if I didn't have to."

A sigh escaped me despite my best efforts. "You do know that time spent with me while I'm asleep doesn't really count, not from a relationship standpoint."

Crap. I'd just said the 'r' word.

"Maybe not for you, but it does for me. I'll take whatever I can get."

I felt my cheeks heat up. Alec reached over almost as if to take my hand before he thought better of it.

"I really wish I could take you with me."

"Yeah, I don't suppose that would work, not now that Mom's back."

He hesitated, on the verge of saying something before shrugging. "In good news, Christmas is just around the corner."

I put my head in my hands. "Somebody needs to teach you the meaning of 'good' news."

"For your information, I have it on good authority that most people do think the arrival of Christmas is a good thing. Rachel goes positively giddy at the thought."

"That's just because it's the perfect opportunity for her to spend obscene amounts of your money on people who can't refuse her gifts without looking like Scrooge."

"True. Despite all that, the arrival of Christmas wasn't the actual good news." Alec paused, as if he needed the dramatic flair to keep me hanging on his every word. "I've booked a holiday for us. Skiing in Aspen. You, me, Rachel, Donovan, my mom, your mom. All of us."

I felt my eyebrows reach for the sky. "Alec, you can't do that. What about the rest of the pack?"

"I've booked them trips to a wide array of locals. Mostly warmer and widely dispersed, geographically speaking. I think everyone could use a bit of a break from each other."

"But the cost. I mean it's way too…"

Alec cut me off. "It's that or I stop trying to be a restraining influence on Rachel. I mean, you think she's bad now, but really you haven't seen anything yet."

I was fumbling for excuses now. "My mom. I mean she'll never go for it. I don't even know how I'd broach something like that with her."

Alec smiled again. "Don't worry about that. I'll ask her. In fact that's part of why I told Rachel I'd drive you home today. This way I can meet her and start the wheels turning for our trip."

We'd just turned off the road and I felt my stomach drop as my house came into view. Mom had been worried enough about me dating Brandon. She'd flip at the thought of another rich, gorgeous boy dating me…wanting to pay for expensive trips for us.

"I don't think that's a good idea. I mean I do want you to meet my mom, but I think it would be best if I had a few days to prep her."

"I don't think that's the way to go here, Adri. I mean she's bound to see me drop you off. That's going to tip her off, and then I'll look less than honorable."

"Alec. Please trust me. I need some time to prep her before something like this is even remotely possible."

He had that look in his eye. He was going to fight me on this. I gave him my best puppy-dog eyes. A few seconds later he sighed. "I still think it's a bad idea."

"Thank you."

Flush with success at having brought Alec around to my thinking, I watched him pull down the lane until he disappeared around the corner.

Mom was standing at the window waiting for me, and she didn't look amused.

Chapter 6

Alec Graves
5 hours previously

It was always a nightmare getting Sam off by himself. On the one hand I understood where the three of them were coming from. Sam, Jack, Alison, they'd all been through hell. In Brandon's pack you could never be sure that a dominant getting you off by yourself wasn't a prelude to getting the stuffing kicked out of you or worse.

In that kind of environment the submissives pretty much had to band together into miniature power blocs that had half a chance of avoiding the worst of the excesses. Still, they'd been with us for long enough now to know I wouldn't put up with that kind of stuff even had the rest of the pack been so inclined.

Based on that and the fact Sam knew exactly what it was I wanted to get him off to talk about,

I had to assume he was trying to avoid the discussion. By the time lunch rolled around I'd decided to force the issue.

A quiet word with Isaac pretty much guaranteed that Jack wouldn't be offering to come along when I told Sam we were leaving the campus for lunch. I'd done everything I could to guarantee Isaac wouldn't kill Jack in his sleep or anything, but since the animosity wasn't going anywhere, I might as well get some use out of it. It was certainly making my life extra hard to compensate.

Alison was a lesser concern. She wasn't very good at reading the subtext in most conversations. If it wasn't for Jack and Sam she probably wouldn't have survived a year in Brandon's group. As long as I waited for Rachel or somebody to get her talking about shopping I had known I could slip away with Sam and she would hardly notice.

I led Sam over to my Porsche and then drove us over to Kostas' so we could get a sandwich while we talked. Luckily the place was pretty much deserted.

"What do you want, Alec?"

"You know exactly what I want. I want you to give up the Georgia contact."

Sam jumped a little. It was starting to look like he was either completely stupid or the most accomplished liar I'd ever met. Living with shape shifters generally conditioned you to tell the truth. Not many of us could lie with both our scent and pulse.

"I don't think that's fair. I've been more than helpful when it's come to helping you snatch up the rest of Brandon's assets. Heck, without me you would have been in the dark."

I shook my head. "We already knew about every holding and operation you've told us about. We would have had a harder time in a hostile takeover situation, but we still could have picked them all up and turned a hefty profit over the next couple of years."

"Fine, you and Donovan are omniscient. Why do you need me?"

"Let's cut the crap. You've been trying to let on that you were only peripherally involved with Brandon's holdings. I haven't believed it for a moment. Brandon was never out of contact long enough to be taking a really active role in managing the pack's tithe. You, on the other hand, have entirely too much lip for someone who supposedly spent his entire life at the bottom of the food chain. You've been running the financial side of things for at least the last three years."

"Okay. It was me. Can you blame me for keeping my head down? You and Donovan were always right on our tails and you had ten or fifteen times the working capital we had to play with. I fought tooth and nail to keep you from absorbing us financially because my and Alison's safety depended on it."

I unwrapped my sandwich to buy time while I decided exactly how much of what I knew to place on the table. "No, you did what you did because you enjoyed it and it brought you power. More importantly, while you may have ended with one-tenth of our holdings, you started out with somewhere around two percent. That's astonishing growth by almost any yardstick I can imagine."

Sam leaned back, smiling at the perceived compliment. "That's exactly why you should go ahead and let me run the Savannah group. I'm good at this kind of stuff."

"What's the prime rule of finance?"

"I don't know; whoever has the gold makes the rules?"

"No, the prime rule of finance is that you can only grow as fast as the rate of return on your capital unless you have outside funding."

I thought I detected a slight blip in Sam's heart rate. A good liar yes, but not a perfect liar still.

"In layman's terms, your nest egg didn't double nearly three times in three years without either someone else loaning you a whole heap of money or experiencing the kind of growth that is almost never found in legal endeavors. Probably both."

"I don't know what you're talking about. The Georgia group is completely above board. I ran a lot of the business, but Brandon kept his hand in some. That's where the real growth was."

I slipped my hand under the table, shifted it over to nine inches plus of retractable claws, and sank a couple inches into Sam's leg. "You're lying. The so-called Savannah group isn't even based in Savannah. We tracked Vincent over to Savannah three times and the round trip time between when he dropped out of sight and when he resurfaced was perfect for Charleston."

Sam was sweating now, very obviously fighting the urge to squirm, which would just drive my claws further into his leg. He opened his mouth, likely to lie again, but I cut him off.

"The profit we'll turn on the holdings we've swept up in the last couple of weeks will undoubtedly come in handy at some future date, but that's not the only reason we've been interested in Brandon's old activities. Donovan and I have been hunting down your illegal golden goose."

When lying didn't work Sam turned to anger. It was a useful piece of information.

"I brought a lot to the table when we offered to join you. We could have gone to any number of different packs and been treated like royalty based on the amount of money we could produce. I could still do that. I'm sure the Coun'hij would be very willing to cough up a million dollars as seed money knowing that I could double it inside a year."

I shook my head again. "There's been a bank error. All of your assets have been frozen. You won't make it very far, especially if you drag Alison and Jack along with you."

I let Sam process that fact. I was pretty sure he had the odd fifteen grand hidden here and there, but he had to know most alphas would just torture him for the information and then discard him once they had it.

"I want a name and a location, Sam. You've been running something illegal and it needs to stop."

Sam sighed, rubbing his wrist where James had thrown him into a table earlier. "Okay, it's illegal, but it's not a big deal. The contact distributes marijuana, but those kinds of deals are always cash at the time the transaction goes down. Our guy is pretty successful but he likes to spend his earnings, so every time he looks to expand we're the ones that he turns to for financing."

I let the silence radiate out, watched it work on him. I wasn't surprised when he was the first to break it.

"Look, could you please let go of my leg? I swear I'm telling the truth."

"Fine, give up your contact and everything will be okay. Refuse and you're going to find out just how unpleasant I can get."

Chapter 7

"Adriana Paige. You can't really think I'm going to believe that!"

"It's the truth, Mom. We just started hanging out together. It's nothing, we're just really good friends."

I'd known Mom would freak out about the idea of Alec taking us on a trip. I hadn't expected she'd be so concerned about my having a new guy friend. We'd been arguing for the last ten minutes and it was starting to look like Alec had been right.

"You're lying to me. Don't tell me you're not, I can tell."

I opened my mouth to protest and she cut me off again. "You obviously like him, and based on the way he was looking at you, he's very much attracted to you."

That made me pause. It was so easy to forget Alec really liked me. Without outside reminders

I was always talking myself into believing it was a temporary thing for him.

"What have you been up to while I've been gone? He's probably been over every night."

I shook my head emphatically. "Mom, I can promise nothing has happened that you need to worry about. It's true that I'd like for Alec and I to be more than we are. He's really a good guy."

"Alec...Alec Graves?"

I hadn't expected Mom to know his last name. That didn't seem to bode well.

"Yes, he's Rachel's brother."

"Sweetie, I really liked Rachel, but the Graveses have more money than is healthy for any six families. Everything I told you regarding Brandon goes double for Alec. Boys like that just aren't sincere about things. They grow up learning how to manipulate everyone around them."

"Mom. You were right about Brandon, okay? Alec is completely different though. That's why he and Brandon never got along. Alec is an incredibly thoughtful, mature guy who always does the right thing."

Mom shook her head again. "What kind of boy dates a girl without coming in and meeting her parents? I mean, really."

"First of all, we're not dating. Not really. Second of all, Alec wanted to come meet you just now but I convinced him not to. I wanted to prepare you for the idea first."

"Adri, you wouldn't have worried about preparing me if there wasn't something to prepare me for. This is more serious than you want to let on. I have half a mind to ground you just to keep the two of you apart."

I collapsed so fast I didn't even realize I was falling. When I came to again, my mom was pacing back and forth with her phone in her hand. It was such a familiar sight. It'd been so long since I'd really had panic attacks I'd nearly forgotten our highly-practiced responses.

"Adri…ana. Are you okay? I should have been more careful. I guess I've gotten out of the habit of calling you by your full name. Too much time away at photo shoots."

I groggily pushed my way back onto my hands and knees. "It's okay, Mom. Please believe me though. There's nothing going on with Alec and me that you need to worry about. He'll come over so you can meet him and you'll see what I mean. Until then, can you please not freak out?"

I could see the decision making itself in her eyes. She couldn't keep me away from Alec. Not all the way, not as long as we went to the same school. She could forbid it, but unless she was ready to move again there wasn't much she could do to enforce her decree.

"Okay, sweetie. I'll trust you for now. I just don't like the way that you don't have any other friends. It's not healthy to get too attached to one boy at your age."

"Oh, that has changed while you were gone. I've got Rachel as a friend and a few other kids. In fact Sam and Alison asked me if we could all go to lunch together on Saturday."

Mom blinked slightly, almost as if having a hard time believing that I really had other friends. "Oh. Well then, that's good news. I'm glad to hear that you're branching out. What ever happened to Britney?"

"We don't really talk now. It turns out she was really jealous when we thought Brandon liked me. She said some things, I said some things. I don't think we'll be spending time together anymore."

Mom nodded, but she'd picked up her camera and started absently fiddling with it. There was no surer sign that Mom had moved on to thinking about another project.

Chapter 8

School was every bit as depressing and desolate as I'd expected with Alec gone. I'd been so smug thinking that Mom couldn't keep me away from him, all the while forgetting that he was going to be halfway across the country.

Jasmin was getting more frustrated by the minute. Apparently her efforts with Ben really weren't going well. That didn't help the ongoing tension at lunch. With Alec gone there was less effort to present a unified front to the rest of the world. We all still sat together, but the conversation was more strained. The old pack sat on one side of the table and new pack sat on the other, with Rachel and me sort of in the middle.

Rachel spent more time talking to Jasmin and the others from the old pack. I spent more time talking to Alison and Sam.

I drifted through the last half of the week, coming awake again Friday afternoon in tutoring. Friday was never a big tutoring day. I know—hard to believe kids our age would choose to procrastinate studying a few extra days.

By the time my shift hit, there were exactly three people in the lab: me, Rachel and a strangely familiar boy. As soon as Albert and Peter left the lab, Rachel casually walked over to my table.

"That's Ben. It's maybe our only shot. Who knows what Jasmin had to do to get him here."

I consciously forced myself not to look at him. "Okay, so we need to convince him that Jasmin likes him, that she's for real?"

"Yep. Only by we, we mean you. I've had a go at Ben. A few months ago, it didn't go well."

"Gee, thanks. That's not a lot of pressure or anything."

Rachel turned to leave and then paused, a faraway look on her face. "He really is a good guy, Adri. One who takes secrets very seriously. I think you could tell him pretty much anything and not worry about it getting out."

I let Rachel go back to her table, waited a couple of minutes and then stood up. I felt like a deer on the interstate. I wasn't any good at talking to boys. Heck, I still couldn't really talk to Alec sometimes and we are about as in love as two people could get.

"Hi. Ben, is it?"

He looked up for a second, met my eyes and shrugged. "It's not exactly a secret."

Feeling incredibly forward, I sat down in the chair next to him. "Since it's down to just you and Rachel, I thought I'd come by and see if you had any questions."

"Right. You just happened over. Come on. You rich chicks are all in this together, and Rachel is the queen rich chick."

"It sounds to me like you don't know Rachel very well. You definitely don't know me. I'm about as poor as they come."

"Except now you're rolling with Rachel and Alec so you're getting plenty of perks."

My resolve to help Jasmin was wavering. Not that I didn't want to help, but I was starting to think maybe he didn't deserve her.

"Look, I don't know what got you so bent out of shape, but Rachel's one of the best people I know. Sure, she buys people stuff, but she's not trying to buy friends or anything, she just likes people to be happy. And Jasmin, Jasmin's stood by me when nobody else would. She's risked losing stuff, big stuff to do the right thing. How many people do you know who really care about right and wrong?"

He was ignoring me again, working on some kind of portable video game player. He already had it disassembled into smaller pieces than I knew was possible. He shrugged as he pulled apart two circuit boards.

"Okay, let's say I believe you really mean what you said. Even so, it still doesn't matter if we're from such different frames of reference that the words mean different things to us."

"What, like good doesn't mean good somehow?"

"More like loss doesn't mean loss. For you or me losing a couple hundred bucks would be the end of the world. For someone like Alec he'd misplace ten times that amount and never even blink."

He'd said it all still without looking up. It should have made his statement the kind of casual thing people blow off without even thinking about it. Instead it sent me reeling. His words seemed to mix with Rachel's advice from earlier and I found myself settling back down into my seat.

"Okay. I'll tell you about loss. Last year my dad and sister left home to come pick me up from school. I waited for like an hour and a half, getting more and more pissed by the minute when they didn't show up on time. I remember borrowing a friend's cell phone so I could call home and leave a nasty message on the machine. Turns out they were broadsided by one of those monster SUVs yuppies buy just because they can."

I hadn't examined my memories of that day in a very long time. They hadn't become any weaker. Tears still gathered at the corner of my eyes, and my breathing sped up, but over the last few weeks I'd somehow gained the ability to go through it all without collapsing. Sometimes.

"I was the last one to find out. Mom got the call, tried the school office once, and then went to the hospital. She finally got a hold of one of the neighbors who offered to pick me up and bring me to the hospital. They…well, they were both dead pretty much on impact. It just took the doctors a couple of hours to get around to agreeing with what the universe had already decreed."

Ben had stopped fiddling with the Gameboy. He opened his mouth but I cut him off.

"So now you know the truth. Adriana Paige's attacks aren't some romantic tale about a semi-pro soccer player. Half my family was wiped out between one heartbeat and the next, and I've been pretty much a wreck ever since."

"I—I didn't know. I mean I figured the rumor was pure crap but I never would have guessed the truth."

"It's okay. It's not like I expect strangers to treat me differently or anything. Just remember that it's Rachel, Jasmin and the others who've put me more or less back together. There was nothing in it for them, but they did it anyways. That's not the kind of thing shallow jerks do. I don't know when or how you decided they were pond scum, but you're wrong."

Ben cocked his head slightly to the side. "Okay, you've convinced me. At least partly. So assuming that Jasmin isn't a blood-sucking uber-biotch, what next?"

"Are you asking me for advice?"

"Sure. Jasmin says she likes me, and to be honest I like her too, what I know of her that is. Still, you don't just tell a super-hot girl something like that. I figure another hot girl would be the way to go. Birds of a feather and all that."

I rolled my eyes at his implication that I was anywhere even close to as attractive as Jasmin. "Well, I think the best place to start would be for the two of you to actually spend some time together."

"Please. Can you see Jasmin and me sitting together over dinner on a normal date?"

"Sure, why not?"

"Neither of us is exactly overly talkative. We'd just end up sitting in silence. Besides, I think you learn more about people from how they treat others, not just how they treat you."

"Actually I agree. So what are you proposing, some kind of group date?"

"No, just a bunch of...potential friends hanging out. You and Rachel seem particularly invested in seeing Jasmin and me together. I think the four of us should do just fine."

Chapter 9

Alec Graves
Charleston, South Carolina

By the time I called Donovan, I was well and truly pissed. I had to make a conscious effort not to take it out on him.

"The name Sam gave me was a mule, Donovan. I had to spend like Rachel in Vegas to get it, but I've got the name of the guy behind the operation. Fredric Sergen."

"I'll run the name past our contacts in the southeast, sir. We're particularly thin east of the Mississippi obviously, but I should be able to get something back for you in the next half day or so."

"Don't bother. It's as bad as we expected. Sergen runs every type of drug known to man and my bet is he's responsible for the sharp rise in overall crime in the last three years."

Donovan was silent for several seconds as he ran through the logic trees I'd already spent the last few hours considering.

"Sam was pressing very strongly for money. If we cut Sergen off from the capital flow he's used to and put the word out he's experiencing difficulties, it may bring about the kinds of reverses required to bring him down."

"This isn't the kind of thing I'm willing to leave to chance. Brandon funded this guy because we weren't strong enough to keep him from breaking off in the first place. This is our mess and it has to be cleaned up."

Donovan took a deep breath, more in resignation than acceptance. The problem with raising the kind of child that could one day lead a shape shifter pack is that at some point *they* are the ones deciding what kind of risks they ran.

"I'll contact Alexi. He can have a couple of men there inside of twenty-four hours. It's not a pack matter so there's no reason not to bring in professionals as backup."

"No, Sergen will never let me in sight of him with the kind of backup Alexi will send. I'll have to go in alone. I need you to arrange a withdrawal with a bank down here. A million dollars is about the most that can be carried easily. Do we have that much in liquid funds still available after sweeping up the rest of Brandon's old holdings?"

"Yes. Just barely, but we do have it."

"All right, tell Rachel no crazy shopping trips until I'm back."

"Of course, Master Alec. Please do be careful."

Sixteen hours later I had the rented car drop me off in front of a nondescript building down in the harbor area. The driver hadn't even batted an eye when I'd given him the address. I tried not to think too hard about what kind of business Sergen was running at the location; something that was drawing the kind of moneyed clientele in the habit of renting limos, obviously.

Rather than the tattooed thug I was expecting, an attractive thirty-something woman answered the door. I jiggled the titanium briefcase holding the money and she nodded and led me up a series of stairs to a comfortable room which overlooked the inside of the building. The elegant furnishings inside the room were a stark contrast to the gritty industrial building interior visible through the windows.

The hostess waited for me to survey the room and then cleared her throat. "My name is Jenny. While you're here please don't hesitate to let me know of any need you might have. I'll just go check now to see where Mr. Sergen is."

I'd only been sitting for a minute before Jenny returned. "I beg your pardon, Mr…?"

"Worthingfield."

"Ah yes, Mr. Worthingfield. I must apologize, Mr. Sergen has run into some unexpected delays and will be unavailable for the next two hours."

I felt my face tighten up. I could recognize a power play as well as the next person. Sergen was trying to establish who was calling the shots.

"Our appointment was for now. If he's uninterested in honoring our arrangement I can always take my money elsewhere."

The fear that flashed across Jenny's face was immediate and genuine. She was terrified of what would happen to her if I walked out the door without Sergen getting his money.

"Please, sir. I'm sure Mr. Sergen will be along just as soon as he's able. In the meantime I'd like to offer you some entertainment. If you'd like to describe your preferences I'll make sure you have your pick of the girls."

My knuckles tightened on the titanium case. There'd been rumors of underage girls being imported into the area, but I'd hoped even Brandon wouldn't stoop so low.

Jenny cleared her throat, clearly worried at my lack of response, but her pulse and scent told a different story than the disinterested madam worried only about the displeasure of her boss. There was something almost maternal about what I was getting from Jenny, which made what she was doing worse in some ways.

It was all too much. The briefcase handle bent with a groan. I stood and walked over to

Jenny, pinning her against the wall by her throat. "I think you actually care for these girls a little, so I don't want to hurt you, but if you scream out or lie to me things will go badly. Where's Sergen?"

Jenny started talking very quickly. Funny how people being kept in line only through fear tend to turn on you the first chance they get. I left her tied up so she couldn't call for help and exited the room.

The cozy suite of rooms I'd been in led directly back into the unfinished interior of the building. Apparently there was another set of rooms on the far side; I just needed to cross the wasteland of post-industrial refuse to get there.

I found the two huge bruisers I'd been expecting earlier outside the room just where Jenny had promised. Sergen apparently had decided to amuse himself while he waited. The closer guy, a huge islander wearing a shoulder holster over his white tank top, stepped forward to block my way.

"No tourists allowed. Turn around and go back the way you came."

"Can't. I have an appointment with Sergen."

"He's busy."

I casually slammed the palm of my hand into his sternum. For all the ease of the motion, it carried enough force to knock him back into the wall in a rain of sheet rock.

I'd already turned towards the second bodyguard, a skinny white guy, but he moved faster than any human I'd ever seen before. I flipped my briefcase into his arm. It hit with a sickening crunch as his gun discharged into the ground at my feet.

I expected the second guard to fold up around his shattered appendage, but he went for his backup gun as he was still falling toward the ground. I could hear footsteps as Sergen's other men on site were alerted by the gunfire.

The guard got a shot off as I kicked him. An awl of fire burned through my side as the guard hit against a concrete pylon.

I gathered up the fallen gun and hit the door to Sergen's room with my shoulder, splintering it as I went through. The room's three occupants were in various states of undress. I ignored the first girl, focusing instead on Sergen and the gun he had pressed up against the second girl's head.

"Who the hell are you?"

The hostage was a slender redhead whose eyes had all but rolled back up inside her head in fear. She was at least a couple of years younger than me and my jaw clenched as I took in the numerous bruises dotting her arms and face.

He was getting jumpy. Only seconds until his men would come flooding into the room, and he was losing his nerve. I only had a heartbeat to decide on a course of action. I let the handgun drop.

Chapter 10

Despite having told Mom that I had more friends than just Alec and Rachel, I was pretty stunned by how fast my calendar had filled up. Aspen with Alec, lunch with Sam and Alison, dinner, sort of, with Ben and the crew.

Being busy with friends was pretty much foreign to my existence. It had seemed to reassure Mom though. Obviously if I had that many friends and she hadn't seen Alec since, I must not be in some kind of nightmare co-dependent relationship.

Not only had Mom not freaked out about my Saturday lunch appointment, she'd actually been excited to hear that I was going to the Funcade with Rachel, Jasmin and Ben. I hadn't talked to her about Aspen yet. I was pretty sure the parental leniency was only going to go so far.

Sam and Alison arrived as I was running through Mom's latest batch of pictures with her.

"Hi, guys, this is my mom. Mom, Alison and Sam."

Alison swept into the house and waved at my mom. "Hi, Mrs. Paige. We've heard a lot about you. How was Europe?"

"Exhausting. They kept me so busy with shoots it was all I could do to drag myself back to my hotel room each night. I didn't see much in the way of sights, but it was good experience."

I swung the door shut behind Sam and cleared my throat. "Do you guys mind waiting for just a minute? Mom and I were just about finished running through the stuff she shot yesterday. She hates it when I bail midway through, says it ruins her artistic vibe."

"Don't be silly, dear. I don't expect your friends to just sit around. We've already been through most of the decent stuff. Don't let me hold you up."

Sam smiled earnestly. "Actually, Mrs. Paige, we'd love to see some of your work. Were you shooting in Zions again?"

"I was. There's a spot just west of Angel's Landing that I've been trying to catch in the right light almost since we arrived."

We all crowded around Mom's laptop.

"What about this one, Adri?"

"I don't know, Mom. I think the birds actually ruin it. If you sell it as a smaller print they look like smudges and even with a larger print they're kind of asymmetrical, not in a good way."

Sam shook his head as we finished and Mom set her laptop down. "That's amazing. I mean it isn't very often you get to sit in on a piece of the creative process like that. You're really good, Mrs. Paige."

Mom blushed slightly. "Thanks. I'm still a long way from being where I need to be but I do appreciate the flattery. Careful, Alison. Sam seems like he could be quite the heart-throb."

Alison chuckled. "Oh, he's good, but not nearly as good as he thinks he is."

"I guess we can't all be Casanovas like Alec."

Sam said it with a smile, but there was an edge to his eyes. I was so busy wondering if he and Alison had been fighting lately that I was halfway to the door before I realized Mom's expression had become just the slightest bit fixed.

"You know Alec well, Sam?"

"Yeah. As well as anyone really knows him I guess. He's kind of a private kind of person."

I never would have believed that things could go bad this quick. Whatever had Sam bent out of shape would have to be addressed later. For now I just needed to get him out of the house before Mom completely freaked out.

As if reading my mind, Alison punched Sam lightly in the shoulder. "Alec's a good guy and you know it. Not many people would take in the Dominics and Jasmins of the world like he has."

Mom's expression didn't unfreeze much, but I figured nothing I could say would really fix things right now.

"Shall we head out, guys?"

There was exactly one fast-food place in Sanctuary, and it was surprisingly empty for a Saturday. I managed not to say anything until we made it to Big Al's.

"What is up with you today, Sam? You do remember that I'm dating Alec, right? After that comment, it's going to be that much harder to convince my mom that Alec's not some kind of monster."

"No pun intended, right?" Alison had the grace to look abashed, but Sam's words weren't the apology I was expecting.

"I'm serious. My mom was already freaked out. She's got this thing against rich guys."

"You're right. I shouldn't have said that. Things are just getting pretty bad with Alec gone. The dominants are all riding us pretty hard. Alison is little more than a slave, fetching and carrying for Isaac and Jess."

Alison put a hand on Sam's arm. "That's not entirely fair. We're shape shifters; that's how things work. Dominants boss the submissives around."

"Right, which is totally in keeping with Alec's squeaky-clean image. If anything it's worse that we're being treated like that here. I thought we'd finally be beyond this crap."

I grabbed a French fry while I stalled for time to think. "I thought things were a lot better since you guys came over from Brandon's pack."

Sam shrugged. "It's all relative. We get the crap kicked out of us no matter where we go; Alec was just more misleading about what we were getting into."

Alison looked for a second like she was going to interject something, but instead looked down and grabbed a fry of her own.

I shook my head. "That doesn't sound right, doesn't sound like what Alec is trying to do."

"Maybe you're right, maybe he isn't trying to do that to us, but that's what's happening. Even Jasmin has been riding us lately, and she has less reason than anyone. I know Jack is kind of a maniac, but none of us has done anything to her."

"I'll talk to the others. No promises, but we've been through a lot together so maybe it will help."

Sam smiled. "Thanks, Adriana. By the way, good luck helping Jasmin catch Ben. He seems like a pretty hard sell."

Chapter 11

Alec still wasn't back in town by the time Monday rolled around. I was starting to feel jittery and tired. Someone else might have taken that as evidence Alec really was right about the whole Ja'tell bond thing. I knew I was just missing him. A bad day with Alec beat a good day without him.

Lunch seemed tenser even than the week before. I thought about it for most of the next two classes, but couldn't decide if things were really worse, or if I was just reading into it more because of my lunch with Alison and Sam.

The one bright spot all day was the fact that Rachel and Jasmin were coming over for a strategy session after school. Capture Ben indeed. It wasn't the kind of thing I'd ever expected to get involved in, let alone look forward to, but I actually was looking forward to it.

Rachel waited around for me to finish up my session at the tutoring lab.

"I feel bad that you have to wait for me every day."

"Please. If I wasn't in the tutoring lab I'd just be home doing some other homework assignment. This way not only do I get the assignments done that I'd otherwise be tempted to procrastinate, but I also get to hang out with you."

"And drive your new car?"

"It's true. If I didn't have the excuse of needing to drop you off, then I'd probably have to carpool in with everyone else."

I shook my head as we turned down my lane. The Jeep, and therefore Mom, was gone but Jasmin was waiting for us. I unlocked the door and we all settled into the living room.

Jasmin absently handed me a small package. "Alec sends his regards."

"He's back?"

"No, he's unavailable still, but he was asking about the necklace he gave you last week. I told him you hadn't been wearing it. He thought maybe the chain that came with it was the problem."

I pulled the paper off the small box and found a small silver chain that was even more delicate than the one that'd come with the glass pendant.

I closed the box back up and sighed. "I wish he'd get back here. I miss him."

Jasmin pulled out a notebook and shrugged. "He'll get back when he gets back, but for what it's worth I wish he were back too. The terrible trio need their butts kicked again."

The comment was too reminiscent of what Sam had told me on Saturday. "I don't understand why you guys are so hard on them. I mean sure, Jack is a psychopath, but Alison and Sam don't deserve what's happening to them."

"Don't be so sure. Besides, it isn't a matter of deserving it or not. They are throwing off the power dynamic in the pack. They were small beans in Brandon's pack, but not all the way at the bottom of the totem pole like they are now. Until they accept that's their new place it's just going to cause problems."

"Why does it have to be like that though? Just because they are smaller and weaker doesn't necessarily mean that they deserve to run errands for James or serve as a punching bag when he has a bad day."

Jasmin frowned. "I don't make up the rules, Adri, that's just how it is. Trying to turn the pack into some kind of democratic knitting circle is just going to make things worse in the long run."

"Worse for everyone, or just worse for the dominants?"

"For everyone. Shape shifters aren't civilized. Not really. In our world you have to be able to back things up with violence and muscle. The pack could come under attack at any time. If the best fighters aren't running the show then what incentive do they have to defend the weaker pack members when everyone's lives are on the line?"

I looked to Rachel for help but she refused to meet my eyes. "You stood up for me despite the fact that I'm not any kind of asset to the pack."

For a second it seemed Jasmin wasn't going to respond. "No, Adri. I didn't stand up for you at all. I backed down because Rachel stood up for you. More importantly, I backed down because Alec was willing to die for you and I knew we couldn't survive without him."

"So it wasn't selflessness at all, it was just more dominance in action?"

"I'm afraid so. You're my friend now, but back then it was simply the natural result of the strongest member of the pack sticking up for you."

"Right. I'll keep that in mind."

Rachel came over and hugged me, but Jasmin wasn't done. "Adriana, I know Alec has been shielding you from most aspects of pack life, but you need to understand what he's done. He's essentially put every member of the pack on notice that he'll kill to protect you. It's the same thing he's done with Rachel, the same thing he's done with his mother, and to a lesser extent the same thing he's done with Donovan. The rest of the pack generally all likes those people so it's mostly unnecessary, but it's a factor in why their lives don't suck when James has a bad day."

Rachel had grown silent. She knew what was coming, maybe not in so many words, but it was something she'd probably absorbed with her baby formula.

"Alec having done that makes him vulnerable. It means that those of you he's protecting can be used to drag him into a fight at an inopportune time. Mostly it's not an issue because Isaac backs him up, but you have to be careful not to undercut his authority."

"I haven't done anything."

Jasmin cut me off. "Maybe you don't mean to, but you're doing it. Sam, Jack, Alison, they're all bad news right now. It won't always be that way, but until they settle into their place in the pack that's how it is. Disagreeing with how they are being treated sets you at odds with what Alec wants and weakens him and the pack as a whole."

I felt my face go hard. It was like being told Santa Claus ate a few children each year along with the milk and cookies.

"I don't believe that's right."

Jasmin's eyes bled to the same pale blue Alec's took on before a transformation. "You can choose to ignore the truth but that won't make it go away."

I didn't need Rachel's tightening grip on my arm to tell me I'd pushed Jasmin further than intended. The slight tremor to her clenched fists would've been clue enough.

"I'm sorry, Jasmin. I wasn't trying to call you a liar, I just want… need to believe that there's more goodness in the world than that."

A couple of deep breaths banished the tremble, but it was still the hot eyes of a predator that looked up at me.

"Again, it makes no difference to me, but it will impact Alec. You need to be careful or you'll put him in a position where he's faced with dying to defend you or repudiating you and letting Jack do whatever he wants to you."

Chapter 12

Alec Graves
Graves Estate
Sanctuary, Utah

Jasmin and Donovan found me strapped into the Machine. I hadn't had much time lately to work out and it was making me jittery. Eventually we were going to see some kind of serious opposition and that tiniest extra edge of speed and strength might make the difference. The rest of the pack was convinced my power would save us from anything, but nothing was unbeatable and if Puppeteer got involved we were going to need every advantage to have even a prayer of surviving.

"Master Alec. Is it completely wise for you to be exerting yourself so? There were an alarming number of bullets that Dominic and I spent the better part of last night fishing out of you."

"I'm fine, Donovan. For the most part they're healing up nicely; the bandages just make it look worse than it is."

We both knew he didn't believe me, which was fine as long as he didn't continue to push the issue. I'd never been in much danger. Once I changed to my hybrid form bullets weren't all that great of a threat. Hybrid bodies were just too big, the organs buried under too much muscle for there to be much likelihood of a bullet making it through to something vital.

Of course a headshot could still bring us down, but most people went for center of mass, so their training actually worked in my favor.

Jasmin finally decided to break the silence. "So, are you going to tell me the big secret? As a rule I don't really like lying to my friends."

"Adri liked the chain?"

"Yes. Where have you been all week? Donovan obviously knows, let me in on the story already."

"You know we've been sweeping up all of Brandon's old holdings? Well, Sam's been holding out on us. They had a hugely profitable operation down in Charleston."

Jasmin's eyes got really big. "You do remember that the Coun'hij has declared the east off limits?"

"Under other circumstances I would have honored the restriction, but the 'operation' was a veritable criminal empire. Drugs, extortion, underage prostitution, you name it. It needed stopped."

"So you went and stopped it. Then you and Donovan split up the loot, or not. Why am I here?"

"Sam claims he didn't know the full extent of what Sergen was up to, but I don't believe him."

Jasmin was pacing now. She'd always done her best thinking on her feet.

"So kill him, or at least boot him. We don't want that kind of trash around."

Donovan shook his head. "If you go after him Alison and Jack will jump in. That is the tightest group of submissives I've ever seen. You can't kill one without at the very least injuring the others very severely."

I'd already played that scenario out in my head. Killing Sam was easy. He wasn't even half the fighter Jack was. Dom could probably do it if she were so inclined.

"The problem is that we need some submissives around here. I can do without Sam, but I need the other two as a buffer to keep the rest of us from always being two seconds from throwing down."

Jasmin shook her head. "You need Alison, but you don't need Jack. Jack's more trouble than he's worth."

I looked to Donovan, waiting for his opinion. "I'm not entirely convinced myself of Jack's instability. I've wondered from time to time how much of his aggression is organic and how much of it is Sam prompting him from behind the scenes."

"Okay, you boys may have a point; Sam does do all the thinking for that little trio. Still, it sounds like it's time to take some kind of harsher action where Sam is concerned. He practically has Adri eating out of his hand these days."

I shook my head. "No, we can't do anything overt. For now I just wanted the two of you to know what's going on. I can't tell Isaac or James, they're too close to the issue, and I need some time to come up with a solution that won't turn Adri against me."

"You really think she'd leave you over that piece of crap?" Jasmin shushed Donovan before he could reprimand her for her language.

"I wish I could say no, but the longer I watch Sam in action the more convinced I am that he's smarter than any of the rest of us give him credit for. It looks like he's playing a losing hand, which should be evident to him. The fact he's still playing the game despite that makes me nervous."

Jasmin shrugged. "Okay, I'll leave the intrigue to you two. I've actually got me a date tonight."

"Anyone I know?"

"Please, like I'd tell you."

I waited until Jasmin was safely gone before standing and turning back to Donovan. "You're no doubt curious where the million dollars went."

"The money is yours, Master Alec. It isn't my place to question what you do with your inheritance."

"I'm not going to have that discussion again. Regardless of who the money really belongs to, you're the one who's doing most of the heavy lifting where our finances are involved. You were depending on that money to meet obligations and execute our plans."

"Things will indeed be difficult for a time given the depleted state of our reserves."

"The meeting place I tracked Sergen down to was a brothel. There were nearly thirty girls there, half of them underage. The madam seemed like a half decent person though. He used her daughter to control her. Once he was gone and I'd killed most of his organization, she didn't have any reason to continue to sell the girls."

"The money would be incentive enough for some, Master, Alec."

"She's not that good of a liar. I set up a trust that will make monthly payments to support the girls. They'll be getting regular psychiatric visits too. The two guys you went ahead and had Alexi send arrived just in time to help gather up a chunk of Sergen's assets. It's in a warehouse near Pier 15. Half of it is drugs that will just have to be destroyed, but we can probably recover most of our money out of the cars and the yacht."

Donovan nodded. He might not have felt leaving the girls in Jenny's care was the best option but he knew I trusted him to make it work. He'd set up the appropriate safeguards to help ensure the girls had a chance at a normal life going forward.

"Very good, Master Alec. I'll talk to our factor in Atlanta. He can make arrangements to liquidate the assets."

Chapter 13

"I'm glad you're still coming, Adri."

"You mean despite Jasmin having nearly ripped my head off when I disagreed with her?"

I deserved Rachel's crestfallen look. I really was trying not to overreact to my fight with Jasmin, but it was hard. Funny how the threat of imminent violence could turn the normal spats into something you couldn't just blow off an hour later.

"She's just concerned. She's much closer to the infighting that Alec protects you and me from."

I thought about challenging Rachel's belief in Jasmin's rationality, but it wouldn't change her mind and I didn't want to hurt her feelings. She was too kind-hearted to deserve that kind of venom.

"So Jasmin and I don't see eye to eye. That doesn't mean I'm going to leave her high and dry. Ben was pretty adamant about wanting the two of us there tonight to help defuse any awkwardness. It's not like she tortures kitties or anything, so if I can be there for her I will be."

"Problems, honey?"

Of course Mom came downstairs to catch the very last of the conversation. Thankfully I was getting good at avoiding references to anything out of the ordinary.

"No, Mom. Just the usual teenage girl drama. Jasmin and I had a spat the other day, but she's hoping to catch the eye of one of the boys in school so we're going to meet him at the Funcade."

I'd satisfied her with the first few words. By the time I finished up my explanation she was already thinking about some new location.

"Okay, sweetie. Have fun, but don't stay out too late. It's a school night after all."

"Sure thing, Mom."

The Funcade was the only non-boozing hangout in Sanctuary. It consisted of a collection of arcade games, air hockey and foosball tables. There were a few other games and a limited menu, but it wasn't much to brag about. On the plus side, the fact that there wasn't any alcohol served there meant that my mom hadn't freaked out when I'd told her we wanted to go there. It was truly amazing how Mom could be completely disconnected from the world at large and still know which places were least likely to get me in trouble.

Jasmin was waiting for us in one corner of the parking lot, car door open and music blaring. She nodded at me as I climbed out of Rachel's yellow VW Bug.

"Thanks for coming."

"Just because we had a fight doesn't mean I'm going to smash your dreams."

"Thanks all the same."

She stretched, allowing the white tank top to reveal a dark expanse of taut stomach. Honestly, I still didn't understand why that wasn't all it took to have Ben following her around like a homing pigeon.

"Feels good to be able to just hang around in town without worrying about getting jumped by the other pack."

Rachel laughed. "Right, like you ever let that stop you before."

"Sure, but there's a difference between doing something and doing it while not having to worry about when it's going to bite you on the butt."

We turned and started walking. The steps up to the front door had yellow tape on one side. As we got closer it became evident why. There was bare metal rebar where they'd carted away some of the concrete. It seemed kind of dangerous to me. Tape or no tape.

Jasmin led us up to the door and then paused as if unsure how to proceed. Rachel smiled and stepped around her to get the door. Once we were inside it was easy to spot Ben. He was off at one of the tables, an order of deep fried mushrooms in front of him while he played on the game system he'd been fixing the last time I'd talked to him.

"Hey, Ben."

"Rach, Adri…Jasmin."

Rachel and I made sure Jasmin was directly across from him so they'd get plenty of eye contact, and then we sat down.

"So you got it working?"

"Hmm? Oh, yeah. Later that day. Just took figuring out what exactly was wrong with it. Once you know enough about something it's usually pretty easy to fix it. Help yourself to some mushrooms if you want, guys. They're still warm and this is the only place you can get them in like a hundred miles."

Rachel made some comment about the weather. I took the opportunity while Ben was answering it to unobtrusively size him up. He didn't look particularly good. His sleeves were just short enough that occasionally when he moved you could see the needle tracks. The skin around his eyes was dark and puffy. For all I knew he was high right then but I didn't think so. He was acting too normal. So not high right then, but his last hit hadn't been more than a few days before.

Everything I'd ever been taught told me that Ben was a loser who was going to end up dead before he turned twenty; but the more time I spent with him, the more I could see what Rachel meant.

Ben was a legitimately good guy. When he noticed one of the junior high kids the next table over watching him fidget with the Gameboy he tossed it to the kid without a second thought.

"Enjoy, man. It's an okay game but the real fun was getting it working again. Let's go play some foosball, ladies."

We played foosball, and air hockey, and some car-racing game that Jasmin absently smoked all of us at. I'd almost forgotten what simple, no-strings-attached fun was like. By the time we were inching towards my curfew, things were going really well. We had him opened up and talking about some crazy computer game he'd spent the afternoon playing.

"I'm telling you guys, Zombie Realms is the best way to kill time you'll ever find. I mean there's like a zillion things to do. Grouping, soloing, raiding. We should get a group together some time. There's a free trial account so you could try it out and I've got a couple extra old computers that I fixed up and upgraded just enough to handle the game. If someone has a laptop or something we could all four play at the same time. I mean, if you guys want to."

That last was said looking directly at Jasmin. It was actually pretty cute how into each other they were. Unfortunately Jasmin still wasn't her normal, unruffled self where Ben was concerned. Rachel jumped in before the silence got too awkward.

"Sure, that sounds like fun. I'll bring my laptop and we can all do it. Depending on how many people you can put in a group, if you want we could bring Alec or Dom."

"Sure, bring them both if we can round up machines for them."

We were slowly headed outside, neither Jasmin or Ben willing to hurry our departure. Ben grabbed the door, holding it open for Rachel and me to go through. He followed Jasmin through and I happened to look back just in time to see him trip and start falling.

Jasmin moved quickly, too quickly actually, but he was too far gone, already halfway down to the dangerous rebar by the time she grabbed his arm. Rachel screamed as Ben landed, rusty iron stuck through his thigh.

Rachel and I hurried down the stairs, getting there just after Jasmin who'd jumped, landing gracefully between two of the metal rods. She already had her cell phone out, handing it to Rachel as it started dialing.

Jasmin pulled me down next to Ben so I could support his head and shoulders while she ripped his pants leg away so she could see the wound. Rachel got through to a dispatcher while Jasmin started applying pressure.

"We need an ambulance. Yes, someone's been hurt. At the Funcade."

"Adri, talk to him while I work on this leg. Is he responsive?"

My throat had completely dried up. It took two tries to get the words out.

"Ben, can you hear me? Ben?"

Having something to do focused my mind. First-aid basics started coming back to me. His breathing was shallow. I patted his cheek but got no response.

"I don't know, can't you just get someone here? How much longer?"

Jasmin shook her head. "The EMT's are probably still at least five minutes away. I think it ripped his femoral artery. Direct pressure isn't doing the trick."

I hadn't had the benefit of the anatomy classes that Donovan had forced the pack through, but even so I knew that was serious. If an artery got cut you usually only had seconds before the person bled out.

Jasmin undid Ben's belt and wrapped it around his thigh a couple of inches above the wound. A scrap piece of rebar finished off the tourniquet.

"Rachel, tell them they'll need something to cut the rebar with."

Rachel dutifully repeated Jasmin's instructions as Jasmin pulled my free hand over to where I could keep pressure on the tourniquet. I happened to be looking at Ben's face as she broke contact with him. It went from pleasantly blank to excruciating pain in a heartbeat. As Jasmin picked his arm up to check his pulse the pain faded back away.

The dispatcher interrupted with more questions before I could act on what I'd just seen. "She says to check his pupils. He hit his head pretty hard."

"They're staying dilated. Tell her he probably has a concussion."

My throat had constricted again. "Jasmin, I don't think he has a concussion. At least that isn't all he has."

Jasmin rounded on me with the barest beginning of a tremor to her hands and then forced herself calm again with a visible effort.

"What do you mean?"

"Let go of him for a second."

For maybe the first time in my life I saw Jasmin, always put together and in control Jasmin, go white.

"Jas, I think he's addicted to you."

Chapter 14

The EMT's didn't understand why Ben started thrashing when they pulled Jasmin away from him, but it only took them a second to realize he calmed down as long as she was touching him. They let her stay as they pushed Rachel and me further back so they could get some kind of power tool close enough to cut him free.

By that time a crowd was starting to gather. The owner of the Funcade was among the watchers and I could tell he was thinking 'dead boy' and 'lawsuit' with about equal frequency.

As the ambulance drove away with Jasmin and Ben in it, Rachel handed me her phone. A short while later Mom blessed our trip to the hospital and Rachel and I were on our way.

The hospital was just waiting followed by more waiting. About midnight Mom called

Rachel's phone and told me she'd be excusing me from school the next day. I managed to get permission to stay a little while longer so I could find out what Ben's surgeons said and then went back to waiting.

About a quarter to one I got one of the better surprises of my life. I was lying back in a fairly uncomfortable chair when I heard familiar footsteps. As I opened my eyes Alec pulled me up into his arms.

"You're back!"

"I'm so glad it wasn't you."

"Me too, but I'm worried about Ben. He's been in there for hours and nobody will tell us anything."

Alec nodded and pulled his phone out. "Let me see what we can do about that."

While Alec stepped away to make his call I noticed that Jasmin was awake. Once the doctors had put Ben under there hadn't been any need for her in the operating room so she'd been relegated to the waiting room with the rest of us. She'd curled up on a couch and closed her eyes.

"Hi, Jasmin. Alec is going to see if he can get us an update."

"Doesn't matter."

"What do you mean? We've all been going crazy out here wondering what was going on."

"He's going to survive. I couldn't stop him from falling, not without revealing what I was. I had a second to choose and I chose to obey Alec's orders. I let him fall. I kept him from being impaled through the chest, but in the end it doesn't matter."

"You're not making sense. Of course it matters. You saved his life."

"I saved his life, but addicted him to my touch."

"So? He's addicted to half a dozen other things. That hasn't stopped him from functioning. He'll go through rehab or whatever and get over it."

"It doesn't work like that. You don't know him. The things he can kick he avoids. Best case he'll never speak to me again. Worst case he'll follow me around like a puppy, only it won't be him, it will be the addiction."

I opened my mouth to try and offer comfort, but Alec was walking back over, Rachel a few steps behind him.

"Ben's stable. They've finished repairing the artery in his leg and they're just about done closing him back up."

Whatever Jasmin might have said was cut off by Alec's phone ringing.

"This is Alec."

For the first time in ages I was actually able to hear Donovan on the other end.

"Sir, you'll need to come home now. Your presence has been requested by the Coun'hij. Agony arrived about twenty minutes ago."

None of it made any sense to me, but the very way that Alec's voice became cold and uncaring told me things weren't okay.

"Have they hurt anyone yet?"

"That is a relative concept. Nobody has been…permanently damaged."

"Do what you can to guide Isaac and James through the minefield. I'll be home in ten minutes."

Alec slammed his phone shut and turned to Jasmin. "We're leaving now. Rachel, take Adri home and then meet us back at the estate. Don't dawdle, but call when you're still a couple of minutes away so we can send out an escort. We can't afford a misunderstanding."

Alec's phone was ringing again, but he ignored it, turning to me as he dug a business card out of his pocket. "You have to do exactly what I tell you. Go home and stay with your mom. If she's going to be gone for more than a few hours then call this number and ask the person on the other end to give you a ride into town. Stick to places with crowds as much as possible."

"I don't understand. What's going on?"

Rachel's phone was vibrating now, but Alec refused to be distracted.

"Adri, focus. This is important. Don't spend any time alone that you don't have to. If necessary lie to your mom. If you can somehow convince her to take a weekend down in Vegas or up in Salt Lake, all the better. This is the whole reason I've tried to keep you in the dark. With any luck they'll decide you are a non-combatant and choose to leave you alone rather than suck you deeper into a world you're not supposed to know about."

Rachel held her phone up. "Alec, it's Donovan. He says to tell you that Adri's been specially requested."

"Damn it."

I still didn't know what was going on, my mind was spinning like a bunch of stripped gears, but I was pretty sure I'd never heard Alec swear before. I followed the others out to Rachel and Alec's cars in something very near a daze. A shaking Rachel threw Jasmin her keys and then climbed into the back seat of Alec's Porsche.

Alec had his phone back out. He was talking to someone named Shawn, but I didn't even try to follow the conversation. I'd had too many shocks in too short of a time. Rachel was putting on a brave face but I could tell she wasn't holding up a whole lot better.

As we rounded the last couple of bends before the estate, Alec closed his phone again and turned to me.

"Rachel has an idea how things are going to go down. She's been preparing for this her whole life. Whatever you think you're getting into, though, it's going to be worse than you could possibly expect. Don't speak unless spoken to, don't volunteer any information you don't have to when they do ask you questions, and stay near one of the hybrids. Jasmin will do in a pinch. I'll do everything I possibly can to keep you both alive."

There were two huge guys waiting outside Alec's house when we arrived. I didn't recognize either of them, but there was no mistaking the low-level buzz of shape shifter energy. Jasmin pulled up a second later in Rachel's car.

Alec led us up to the newcomers. "Agony requested our presence, take us to him."

"Right. You know my favorite thing about going out on visits with Agony?"

The shape shifter who had spoken was a black guy with dreads and facial piercings who looked like he could have given Brandon a run for his money in an arm wrestle.

"I don't particularly care why you do what you do, Abaddon. Mostly it just matters that you've chosen to do so."

"Ah, Graves. You're too much like your dad. That's the beauty of things though. You pissant pack leaders all start out so high and mighty, but by the time we leave you always bow and scrape just like you're supposed to."

Alec's fists went white. Whatever he might have said was interrupted by Jasmin.

"I find it equally interesting that someone of your breeding would abandon the position of his pack to go fawn over the Coun'hij. Did you lose any sleep when the Sacramento pack tore your friends apart?"

"Your girl's got a mouth on her, Graves. You should do something about that before she gets hurt."

Alec's smile highlighted the ice in his eyes. "Jasmin's as dominant as they come. She can say pretty much whatever she likes. If you want to call her on it be my guest, but you might want to do your job and get us to Agony before letting her rip your throat out."

Abaddon pointed at the door. "Oblivion, lead the way."

Oblivion looked like a recruitment poster for the Aryan Nations. Blond hair, blue eyes and a complicated web of tattoos up his arms that was oddly surreal. Oblivion looked at Abaddon for several seconds, as if to establish that he wasn't scared of the darker shape shifter, and then turned and opened the front door.

We went through the halls in a clump. Jasmin, then Rachel and I holding hands in a desire for communal reassurance, then Alec with Abaddon taking up the rear.

I'd spent weeks in the Graves manor and still didn't know all of it. We were quickly led to a sub wing I hadn't ever explored, and down three flights of stairs.

The room waiting at the bottom had been carved directly out of the rock the house had been built on. The lighting was provided by a series of candles and torches. The flickering illumination concealed almost as much as it revealed.

Alec took my hand as Abaddon moved around us to stand next to Oblivion. We were another few steps into the room before Alec's hand tightened around mine.

It took a second for my mind to process what I was seeing. Isaac and James were in the front of the group, both sporting a large collection of gashes. I had a split second to wonder how hard you had to hit a shape shifter to make them bruise like that and then my gaze moved on to the other members of the pack.

Jess and Dom had both shifted forms and their normally lustrous coats were heavily stained with blood. Further back, Jack, Alison and Sam had also shifted forms to reduce their vulnerability to attack. None of them had escaped without wounds either.

Andrew and Addison, Jess's father and James's mother looked less the worse for wear than anyone else, but were both trembling with fear. Everyone was scared, but the older pair looked as though they'd already seen this course of events play out and knew the ending was going to be ugly.

Standing almost to the very back of the group was Donovan. The old shape shifter was still in his human form, still unbowed, but the right side of his face was a mass of bruises and blood. The sight drew a gasp from me, but it was nothing on what I felt when I saw Alec's mother lying motionless behind Donovan.

I half started forward, but Alec's grip stopped me from completing the motion. Jasmin was suddenly at my side, between Rachel and me, her voice low. "She's still breathing. She probably freaked out when Agony arrived and had to be tranqed."

Alec pulled us forward until we stood in front of our friends, between them and a slender man who was distinctive in his lack of tattoos or piercings.

"I protest the treatment of my people, Agony."

"It's no less than you deserve for your disgraceful hospitality, young Graves."

"Had you informed us of your coming as tradition requires then you would have found a much different reception awaiting you."

Agony scanned through the pack, starting with Alec and seemingly ending with me. "Oh, but we did attempt to inform you. I had my man call that device you're so fond of. Each time he got a message that your phone was out of service. Once upon a time we would have relied on couriers to provide the necessary niceties, but with you younger leaders we've found modern means to be best."

"Far be it for me to dispute with the Coun'hij or abandon practices which have served our people well for so many years. Please let your fellows know that in the future I'm happy to receive notice via runner. Your man Abaddon, for instance, knows the way here now."

Abaddon moved forward as though to respond to the jab, but Agony stopped him with a gesture. "While that may indeed help avoid future misunderstandings, the fact remains that offense was given. You know our rights?"

Alec went utterly still for the barest instant. "You can demand punishment for those lesser members of the pack which created the offense. Those pack members may in turn demand trial by combat if they feel the punishment is unwarranted."

"Ah, yes. You're quite the scholar of tradition and law, much like your father was before you. It availed him little, much as I suspect it will prove a slight shield for you."

"Tradition and law is all we have as a people to separate us from the animals, all that allows us to constrain our beasts. Even the Coun'hij is bound by the strictures that bind the rest of us."

Agony's dismissive expression didn't fill me with reassurance. If he didn't hold with the laws Alec seemed to be relying on, then what hope did we have?

"I select your Donovan as the worst transgressor. His actions would have been bad enough from any of your people, but coming from one so lowly they were doubly insulting. I had thought I'd taught your mentor better on the occasion of my last visit. It appears the lesson needs to be refreshed."

A barely-perceptible stir of movement ran through the figures behind me as Agony's target was named. Donovan's graceful limp slowly brought him even with me as he moved towards the open space between Alec and Agony.

Despite Alec's order to keep my mouth shut I was halfway to protesting the situation, but Alec tapped my hand and then reached out and stopped Donovan.

"It's your right to demand his punishment, but he stands under my protection. As such, it is equally my right to stand in his place and demand trial by combat. Who will you name to oppose me?"

There was a growl from the cluster of figures behind Agony. For a moment I thought it would pass unremarked, but Agony's sadistic smile argued otherwise.

"I believe there is one among my party who has waited a long time for this opportunity. I trust, young Graves, that you remember Vincent?"

Chapter 15

When Vincent stepped out of the cluster of Agony's men I thought for a moment my heart was going to explode.

It was suddenly like our defeating Brandon's pack had never happened. If anything, Vincent was scarier than I remembered. His eyes were the same dead, psychopathic orbs that'd all but screamed he was through pretending that anyone else's pain mattered in the slightest. He was bigger now though and he moved with an economy of motion that was eerily similar to Alec's movements.

Jasmin's thoughts must have run along the same track as mine. "Look who's back with a graduate degree in sociopathy and all the tricks you'd expect from two weeks of almost constant combat."

Some of my spiking alarm must have made it through to my face, or possibly she just heard my pulse stutter.

"Don't worry. Alec was always able to wipe up the floor with Vincent. Vincent's bigger, but Alec's put on muscle since they last clinched too. Besides, all Alec really needs to do is pop the cork on that little black hole he carries around in his pocket and everyone here will collapse."

Somehow with everything that'd happened since the fight with Brandon I'd forgotten about Alec's power. Maybe it was just that we'd spent so much time needing him to manifest an ability. It was hard to believe it'd really happened, that Alec finally had the ability to keep the pack safe.

Rachel was back with her mom, but the rest of the pack was milling around Alec, creating a rising tide of shape shifter energy. The growing tingle should have been reassuring, but the answering roar of power from the seven figures on the other side of the cavern dwarfed the output of our pack.

As Alec turned towards Vincent I grabbed Jasmin's arm. "Is it to the death?"

"Not necessarily. In theory they fight until Agony deems that the insult has been satisfied or until one of them is defeated."

"In theory?"

"Accidents happen."

Alec handed me his cell phone and then began unbuttoning his shirt. A moment later he was down to his ha'bit and facing Vincent who'd shifted to his hulking hybrid form while Alec was still preparing.

Vincent sent out a pulse of crackling energy which Alec answered with greater power of his own and then they dashed towards each other.

As always they moved too fast for me to follow every motion. Alec shifted to his hybrid form in the blink of an eye and then they were fully engaged. I saw a flicker of movement and then Alec backed away, blood on his claws.

I was able to garner some clues to the fight by watching Abaddon out of the corner of my eye. Every time he frowned my heart rose, every time he smiled I felt a little part of me wilt. It seemed like the two combatants were mostly probing.

The whirling storm of fangs and claws sped up and then suddenly the fight went to the ground. I didn't need the collective gasp from my pack to realize Alec was on the bottom. From everything I'd heard or experienced, I expected Vincent to be ripping away at Alec's body while trying to reposition for a killing hold. Instead they were locked in a kind of stalemate holding onto each other's wrists while Alec's legs had wrapped around Vincent's waist.

Arms that were more than capable of lifting up the front end of a luxury car strained against each other and then slowly they started moving away from Alec, towards Vincent. The first of Alec's claws sank into Vincent's throat and then suddenly Vincent sprang away in an explosion of movement.

I expected them to fall back and regroup but it appeared Alec had managed to keep a hold of Vincent's left wrist. Both hybrids blurred again as they jockeyed for position and then Alec was behind Vincent.

Just to the right of me, Jasmin leaned forward eagerly and I knew Alec had set himself up for the kill. Vincent violently tried to shake Alec off, slamming backwards into a wall and then spinning around, flailing with his claws in an effort to pry Alec free.

Moving so slowly even I could see it, Alec crept up Vincent's back, his hands anchored in Vincent's chest. A split second before Alec's mouth would have latched onto the back of Vincent's neck, Agony moved forward and backhanded Alec into a wall.

"Enough. The offense has been cleansed by battle."

For a second I thought Alec would turn on Agony. Based on the sudden tensing all around me, the rest of the pack had the same worry.

Alec's shape trembled in rage as the man fought with the beast, and then suddenly the hybrid melted away. I didn't see Isaac and James move, it was like they just appeared at Alec's side, ready to support him if needed.

Alec looked over to our pack as though verifying everyone was still okay, and then turned back to Agony.

"The debt is washed clean. Quarters have been prepared for you and your men. I expect you remember where they are?"

At a nod from Agony Alec continued. "All further discussions can take place between you, me and our most dominant members."

"Trying to protect the weaker members of your pack again, Alec?"

"Nowhere does tradition require the entire pack to assemble each and every time we talk. It is my right and I stand by it."

Agony's smile left me feeling cold and dirty. "See to it, Oblivion. Somebody pick up Vincent. I'll see you again after my men have had a chance to settle in, Alec."

After Agony's people had left the cavern Alec had hustled everyone back upstairs. "We don't have a ton of time. James, Isaac, settle your parents back in their rooms. Dom, Jess, Alison, Sam, Jack go with them in case they run into trouble. Donovan, if you could please see to my mother? Jas, Rach, can you please help them?"

The boys had already disappeared, girlfriends and submissives in tow. Jasmin grabbed Alec's arm as he turned away.

"Where are you going?"

"Adri needs to get back home."

Donovan had stopped now too. "Master Alec, Agony won't like that."

"I'm aware of the risks. Adri can't afford to alienate her mom right now though. She's got things she needs to do."

Jasmin opened her mouth to argue, but Donovan turned and started walking away, Alec's mom in his arms.

"I don't know what you mad scientists have cooked up, but we're in too deep to do anything but trust you."

A minute and a half later, Alec and I were in his Porsche. He normally drove fairly sedately when I was in the car with him, but he hit nearly triple digits on the lane before he had to break for the main road.

"Please listen carefully, we don't have much time, and we're still in quite a bit of danger."

Alec down shifted around a corner and cranked his car back up to one-twenty. "We've been worried this would happen for quite a while, but our bringing down Brandon's pack was always pretty much guaranteed to force their hand. I need you to go to Mallory. She needs to be updated on what's going on."

"Wouldn't it be safer for you to do it?"

"No, Agony's men will have us under virtual house arrest. There's too many of us for them to follow everyone."

"I don't even know how to find her."

"Take the road past my house then the first right. Just keep driving until you see the shed. There's an overhang about fifty yards further along. If you get to where the road gets bad you've gone too far."

"What about a vehicle?"

"You'll either have to borrow your mom's or find a way into town and borrow Jasmin's. The key is taped to the bottom of the passenger seat. The combination to unlock it is one-one-two-three-five."

"Fibonacci's sequence?"

"Yeah, we standardized all of the unlock codes on all of our vehicles. It was a safety measure in case something like this happened."

We pulled into my lane. The Jeep was just visible in the darkness.

"Things are going to be okay, right, Alec?"

"I don't know. We've been operating under the assumption that my power would serve as an equalizer against the Coun'hij. That's the only reason we haven't been in a panic since Brandon went down."

"So we're okay then."

"The fight against Vincent was a test. I reached out for my ability and there wasn't anything there."

Chapter 16

Alec Graves
Graves Estate
Sanctuary, Utah

I felt jittery the whole way back from dropping Adri off. I'd hoped to have more time. I'd known since right after I'd killed Brandon that my power wasn't manifesting any more. I'd hoped it was still just in the development stage, that a few weeks would see it come back.

It wasn't the kind of thing I could risk getting around, even to Donovan, so I hadn't mentioned my concerns to Mallory. The one time I'd visited she hadn't said anything so I'd figured nothing had changed as far as she could tell.

To have Agony on our doorstep now, while we were still trying to integrate a third of the pack, was bad news on just about every level.

As I pulled into the garage I got a call from Donovan. "Master Alec. In light of current circumstances I've turned on the motion sensors. It appears as though someone just entered your bedroom. Would you like me to send Isaac and James to meet you?"

There was the rub. No matter how scared we might be individually we had to pretend it was just another day. If we started huddling together like a bunch of scared puppies it'd just be a matter of time before Agony's guys tore us apart.

"No, there's no need. If you could have someone clean the hallway around the corner from the second library I would appreciate it though. I noticed it's starting to look worse for the wear."

"Indeed, sir. I'll have it looked into at once."

It was indeed Agony who was waiting for me inside my room, browsing one of the books from the array of shelves that took up most of my walls. I spared a brief moment to hope that I'd shut the door to my studio before I'd left. It was self-locking, but I occasionally left it open if I wasn't working on anything important. The last thing I needed was to throw Agony any more clues how important Adri really was to me.

"Graves. I was surprised to find out you left rather than see to our comfort."

"I was within my rights. Because of our age, various members of the pack have appearances to keep up with the community. No one asks any questions when an adult is reclusive. When minors aren't enrolled in school it nearly always makes people curious. We considered home schooling, but decided we couldn't get away with it for more than one or two of us."

"Indeed. Appearances must be maintained. I find it interesting that you didn't kill Vincent. I'd understood your hatred for each other to be quite virulent."

He was probing. It'd been inevitable when I didn't use my power, but I'd hoped to have a few minutes to gather myself first.

"You're a member of the Coun'hij. You don't voice idle observations, so I have to assume you're referring to the fact that I kept the confrontation to a purely physical fight."

"Indeed."

"Have you never desired to best someone on their own terms? Vincent has always claimed to be equal to the best the moonborn had to offer. He believes he can take anyone in a straight fight despite having been proved wrong on a number of occasions. I want him to die by my hand and know in doing so that I've bested him on equal terms."

"What a romantic idea. Only two young men, barely more than infants, could possibly hope to perceive the world so."

"Youth does not necessarily equate to foolishness or weakness."

Agony set the book down and moved closer. I fought the urge to tense up. A hybrid with the kind of power I'd displayed in the fight with Brandon wouldn't worry about a physical confrontation with Agony.

"But power doesn't necessarily equate to wisdom. What do you intend to do with your newfound strength, young Graves?"

"For now I wish for nothing more than to be left alone with my friends and family."

"A good answer for a human. You and I know our kind doesn't think like that. Power must be exercised in order to serve as a deterrent. The tales that Vincent has carried are of a wondrous ability that allowed you to knock two large packs to the ground. A power like that would virtually guarantee you a spot on the Coun'hij. Rather than ruling over a pack of foolish youngsters you could sit with my brethren and me and determine the course of our race."

"I have no desire to rule anywhere. A thousand years ago it wasn't uncommon for the most powerful warriors to keep their own counsel. I see no reason to do differently."

"Ah. But things have changed. With the southerners broken, their efforts turned inward towards ruling that snake pit they call home, there's no longer the mortality rate among us there once was. For every functioning pack there are at least two or three loners who've proven too strong to be ruled but not strong enough to rule in turn."

Agony turned his back to me, picking up my physics textbook with a condescending shake of his head.

"I'd hoped to do you a favor. Your killing Vincent in a manner that overwhelmingly proved your superiority before all my other men would have gone a long way towards preventing the kind of unrelenting challenges that are otherwise only a matter of time."

I shook my head. "I'll deal with the dispossessed if and when they show up."

"I guess we'll see. You're either remarkably confident for someone so young, or trying to run a spectacular bluff."

Once Agony left I paced my room for a couple minutes. The wisest thing would be to go to bed, to follow my normal routine, but I didn't think I'd be able to sleep in a room Agony had so recently defiled with his presence.

I debated options for several seconds before heading towards Donovan's study. Agony would have his men monitoring the phones as expected, but there was one phone in the house that didn't route through the closest phone line.

After Agony's first visit, Donovan had paid a small fortune to have a phone line run directly from his office to three separate locations in town. It wasn't the kind of thing that would manage to stop law enforcement, but with the advent of the internet, we'd been able to add one more level of camouflage. Isaac was every bit as good with programming and networking as James was with vehicles. He'd created a device that routed a random set of frequencies through all three phone lines and then added a fourth stream of encrypted data that went out over the internet.

It wasn't perfect, but unless you anticipated where we were calling and got a tap at that end, it was pretty much unbreakable.

I ran my finger over the scanner at Donovan's office door and let myself in. I flipped on the white noise generator, queued up Isaac's program and dialed Shawn's number.

"This is Shawn."

"Hey, Shawn, it's Alec."

"I wondered if I'd get a second call from you today. You've got Isaac's trick going full bore?"

"Yeah. Agony's in typical form. He's got Vincent with him and seems to pretty much be hoping for a replay of the last time he was here."

"That's the rumor we heard last night. I would have called to warn you but by that time I figured there was too much chance they already had your lines tapped."

"How much trouble am I in?"

"If you can replicate the trick you did with Brandon I'd say pretty much none. Just challenge Agony on the spot and kill him."

"Yeah, if I want to end up on the Coun'hij and then spend all of my time trying to avoid a knife in the back."

"There is that. Well, assuming you...don't want to escalate things like that then you're in for a hard road. Even on the Coun'hij there's only a couple of people more powerful than Agony. Puppeteer tops the list. I guess Oblivion could probably take him too, but all indications are that he's as firmly in Agony's pocket as always."

"Do you have any good news for me?"

"Maybe. There's a straw on the wind. I heard some rumors that a few of the Coun'hij enforcers were pissed about being given conflicting orders. Agony initially wanted an extra six or seven hybrids to accompany him, but for some reason cut back on the size of the party a few hours before he left."

"So the other leaders overruled him."

"Right, which probably means two things. He's scared to death of just what you're capable of right now, and the rest of the Coun'hij was worried he was coming to fabricate an incident."

"Not just that. They are worried they won't be able to cover up the incident if he brings an army along."

"Right. It's the first real sign that they are worried about losing control since the last time Agony was in Sanctuary."

"Thanks for the intel."

Chapter 17

Mom had been waiting for me. She'd noticed it was Alec who dropped me off rather than Rachel or Jasmin. I could tell she wasn't entirely buying my story about him having met us at the hospital, but she let me break past and go to my room.

Just before I went to bed I got a single text from Jasmin.

Ben?

I woke up about noon. Mom was already gone. I threw some clothes on and stumbled downstairs. The note on the fridge was like she was reading my mind.

I'll be out until later today. Stay home and get your homework done. I didn't call in to excuse you so you could play all day.

I called the hospital and convinced them to put me through to Ben.

"This is Ben."

His voice sounded different, high maybe?

"Ben, it's Adriana. Jasmin asked me to call and find out how you were doing?"

"Jasmin? Is she there with you?"

"No, she sent me a text."

"I don't understand. Why hasn't she been returning my calls?"

His voice was changing. The dreamy edge was wearing off, there was a hunger growing in it.

"I'm sure she'd like to, but some stuff came up that she has to deal with."

"What aren't you telling me?"

My mind went back to Rachel's words from earlier. "I'm sorry, Ben. I'd like to tell you but it's not my secret to share."

"She's in danger, isn't she? Don't bother answering, I know she is. For her to do something she doesn't want to do pretty much means she has to be. She'd tell anyone who wasn't bigger and badder to just eff off."

"There's a certain element of risk, but you don't need to worry about her. We're working to make sure everything is okay."

"I want to help. What can I do?"

"It's not exactly that kind of..."

Ben's voice was eager now, insistent. "You trailed off. You thought of something."

"I need a ride into town, the Funcade. I know you can't leave the hospital yet, but if you know someone that could help me?"

"Don't go anywhere, your ride will be there in the next half hour."

I was expecting a parent or maybe a grandparent. I wasn't expecting Ben to pull up in a battered, primer-gray Mustang. It looked nothing like Brandon's sleek, new machine but I recognized the insignia.

"How did you convince them to let you out of the hospital?"

"I didn't ask, I just got up, dressed myself and left. I hitchhiked home and grabbed my car."

I climbed into the car and noticed blood soaking through his pants.

"You're bleeding. You could kill yourself if you open your leg back up."

"That doesn't matter. All that matters is Jasmin. We have to protect her; have to make sure she comes back to me. We're supposed to be together."

The engine in the old sports car groaned as Ben stomped on the gas. He was taking the turns almost as fast as Alec had last night, but with less control.

"Slow down. We aren't going to do anyone any good if we get into a wreck."

Ben eased up a little, but kept tapping the steering wheel. It was like they'd given him a dose of meth at the hospital. His words came in staccato bursts like his thoughts were racing away and then stopping abruptly.

"Where do you need to go?"

"The Funcade."

"Jasmin's at the Funcade?"

"No, her car is though. I need to get it."

Ben grabbed a chunk of his hair and pulled until I was worried it was going to come out. "I need to see her."

I'd thought I'd understood what it meant when I'd told Jasmin Ben was addicted to her. I hadn't, not really.

"Ben, listen to me. This isn't like you. I can't explain why, but I think that you're addicted to the sensation of Jasmin's touch."

"No, that's not it. It's love. I know what addiction feels like and this isn't it, it's too strong."

We'd arrived and I hesitated, torn between whatever vital information Mallory might possess and the need to protect Ben from the monkey that'd latched onto him while he hadn't been looking.

"You say you've been through addiction. Really sit down and think about what you feel. It's beyond obsession."

Ben's fists clenched white around the steering wheel. "I think you should get out now."

I slid out of the car and then watched as Ben's Mustang peeled out of the parking lot.

The code worked exactly as promised and the key was where it was supposed to be. I started the Mercedes up, spared a moment to hope I wouldn't crash it, and then dropped it into gear.

As I drove past the estate I saw movement in the underbrush. My stomach dropped down even with my knees, but I didn't have any choice but to just keep going and hope none of the Coun'hij hybrids jumped out in front of the car.

I found the overhang Alec was talking about, parked the Mercedes underneath it and then started hiking in roughly the direction I remembered from my last trip.

When I was nearly ready to give up I started calling out for Mallory. She appeared five minutes later, put a finger to her lips and guided me back to her cabin.

"Well, child. Either you've decided to come here against Alec's orders, or the Coun'hij has sent a group. I don't believe it's the former, so you'd better fill me in on how bad things are."

"They arrived last night. Alec, Jasmin, Rachel and I were all gone. Donovan called and we hurried back, but by the time we arrived their leader was claiming the rest of the pack had disrespected him or something."

"Slow down and start with the basics. How many of them where there?"

"Seven. The leader's name was Agony. There was also someone named Oblivion, one named Abaddon, and Vincent was there too."

Mallory flinched slightly at Agony's name, but took a deep breath and continued. "Why were you there? I wouldn't have expected Alec to expose you."

"He wasn't going to but Donovan said they requested me by name."

Mallory was pacing now, slowly dragging her frail body around the room. "That might not mean anything. Vincent was with them, but that's not his manner of thought. Nobody else is truly real to him, and humans even less so. Tell Alec you may have a spy in your midst. If so it's likely one of the three newcomers."

"No. They're all loyal to Alec."

"Truly, child? You've never heard them express dissatisfaction with their lot? I never liked the thought of bringing them into the pack but Alec was right that we need more submissives. The pack needs an outlet in order to avoid ripping itself apart."

I felt like I'd been slapped down. This was too important to let my feelings get in the way though.

"Agony said Donovan was the worst offender. He wanted to punish him, but Alec stepped in and offered to fight one of them in Donovan's place."

Mallory was smiling now. "Smartly done. It's all a dance to figure out who will blink first, Alec or Agony. Agony immediately put one of the pack under threat of pain, but Alec spoked his wheel by taking Donovan's place."

I nodded. It made a weird kind of sense. "That was when Agony told us Vincent was here and said Vincent would fight Alec."

"Excellent. If Agony had been sure of his ability to defeat Alec he would have taken the challenge right then and broken him. Alec's gamble helped keep the loyalty of his pack and showed them the Coun'hij is bluffing all at the same time. So Alec fought him, tapped into his power, and dropped Vincent where he stood?"

"No, he fought him hand to hand. He won, but it wasn't until after that he told me he tried to use his ability but nothing happened."

Mallory's good humor evaporated. "He told you that? Not where anyone else could hear, I imagine. It's important that the pack not realize how bad our position is."

"Has his power evaporated? Are we vulnerable to whatever other pack comes along?"

"Powers, abilities like the one Alec manifested, shouldn't just go away. It's possible it manifested prematurely in the fight with Brandon and just needs more time to come in fully, or more practice before it will heel when called. I just don't know. It's not a science and almost anything could be possible."

I felt my heart sink but she mustered up a smile for me. "Don't despair. What we need most is more time. Agony used his only truly expendable piece in the fight last night. The rest of his men will all be reluctant to fight."

"I don't understand. Isn't that why they are here?"

"Yes, but generally they don't have to fight and the Coun'hij's enforcers generally take an odd pride in the fact that they don't usually need to fight. You saw the tattoos and piercings?"

"On everyone but Agony and Vincent."

"Those all go away when we change shapes. Generally the more tattoos and piercings one of the enforcers sports, the higher up the food chain they are."

I thought back over the shadowy figures half glimpsed in the torchlight. "Abaddon had the most. Oblivion had relatively few, towards the bottom maybe. Agony had none."

"Agony had none because he is the one who does most of the fighting. He's somewhat unique in that way. Most of the Coun'hij uses their minions. He knows the fear of what he can do is the best weapon available him."

"What does he do?"

"He scars. When he wounds someone he can will them never to heal again. That's how I got like this, how Donovan acquired his limp. Agony rides a thin line between enough terror to keep everyone in line and too much terror, the kind of terror that would cause a general uprising. As long as the packs all feel they still have something left to lose they'll allow him to keep doing what he does."

"Keeping everyone in line?"

"Yes, keeping all of us in line." Mallory resumed pacing. "It's good news that Abaddon is the most freakish. He's an incredible fighter but he doesn't have any kind of special gift. Oblivion is actually a bigger threat. He's the only powerful enforcer who doesn't go in for ostentatious ornamentation. Just enough to keep the new enforcers from giving him grief. It saves him from having to use his power as often."

"What's his power?"

"He steals minds. One moment you're walking and talking. He touches you and you're a blank slate."

I waited while she paced back and forth for several seconds. "So what do I tell Alec?"

"You tell him what he already knows. Bluff for as long as he can get away with it, but when push comes to shove he needs to give Agony whatever the Coun'hij wants. We need time. Time for his power to stabilize or be trained or whatever it is going to take to give the pack a chance to survive."

The fear and anger that had been simmering in the back of my mind since I'd seen Agony came to the fore.

"That can't be the answer. He's going to kill people. He'll hurt them badly at the very least, but I think he's going to kill someone."

"I expect you're right. The question is not how Alec stops him—without his power working right now, the question is do we let Agony kill one person, or do we let him kill the whole pack?"

Chapter 18

Mallory followed me back to the car, dragging some kind of pungent bush behind us to cover up my scent. She extracted a promise to drive further along the road for another half hour before I turned back around and went home. Apparently automobiles didn't have a distinctive enough scent to track unless they were the only one that'd passed by in quite a while.

Normally Alec and Mallory didn't employ that level of deception, but with the Coun'hij delegation in town she was understandably jumpy.

I was still a few minutes away from the estate when two massive shapes suddenly stepped out onto the road in front of me. I managed to come to a stop without running either of them over. When I realized who it was I wished I'd floored it.

I didn't recognize the second shape shifter, but Oblivion was unmistakable. His hulking form crossed over to my side of the car and opened my door, but it was the second man who began interrogating me.

"You're Graves' pet human. You passed by this way a couple of hours ago. Where were you going?"

I felt my mouth go dry. Lying was pointless. They could hear my heartbeat, smell the nervous perspiration gathering on me.

"None of your business."

He didn't even blink and I never saw the backhand coming. He must have really pulled the blow. He could have easily snapped my neck without thinking about it, but it still left my ears ringing.

"You can address me as sir, or Master Marco."

I'd been nervous before, now I was terrified. Marco walked over to me, his right hand shifting over to claws as he got closer.

I opened my mouth, but he wasn't interested in anything I had to say yet. He sank the longest claw into my upper arm. I screamed and nearly passed out, but he kept eye contact with me the whole time.

The sadistic light in his eyes amply communicated that information would be nice, but he was mostly interested in hurting me.

I was shaking now. Shock, fear, pain—it didn't matter the reason, I was suddenly very much aware of just how much trouble I was in.

Marco pulled the claw out of my arm and brought it up towards my face.

"Be a real shame to ruin such a pretty face."

A heartbeat before the point would have raked across my cheek, a tattooed arm grabbed a hold of Marco's hand, effortlessly immobilizing it.

For a second I thought Marco was going to turn on Oblivion, but he glanced nervously at the hand and backed down with an immediacy that was nearly unbelievable.

"Fine, do it your way. I was just trying to save you from getting your lily-white hands dirty. We all know how carefully you conserve your ability."

Oblivion gripped me by the upper arms, locked gazes with me and then suddenly my vision stopped working. I was still trying to orient myself in the black void when I started hearing voices. Each voice was different, most only got one word out before being replaced.

"Stolen...Memories...Leave...Holes...Secret ...Trusting...You."

Before I could fully process the meaning of the chorus of voices, I found myself in another place. My eyes worked, too well in fact. The normal faded colors of near darkness were overlaid with the inner glow of a shape shifter's vision.

I couldn't control my body. Eyes, head, hands, nothing. I was midway through a full-blown panic when I saw Donovan. His face was the same gentle, lined canvas I'd always known, but his leg wasn't injured.

The wonder of seeing Donovan move around without his habitual limp was enough to make my panic jump the tracks. I inhaled and found a hundred new scents. Many of the scents were other shape shifters, rivals by the way my muscles tensed up every time I thought about them.

I scanned the crowd. I'd never seen so many shape shifters in one place at the same time. Gradually I started picking other familiar faces out. Mallory was there, standing tall and regal to the right of a man who looked oddly familiar.

There was Andrew and a little ways over I could see Addison slightly behind a man nearly as big as Brandon had been before Alec had killed him.

I wanted to continue looking at the people but something made me turn and look at my surroundings. We were in a bowl-shaped valley with a stream cutting through one end. My hearing was keen enough to make out the sound of a full-fledged river, likely the ultimate destination of our little brook.

It was autumn, I could taste the slightest hint of chill on the air and the leaves felt like they'd present a riot of colors if it were light enough for their full glory to manifest.

A wiry figure that I quickly recognized as Agony, was talking now. "Your man has crossed too many lines this time, Graves."

"He does what he's done under my order."

"The ancient prerogatives aren't in effect anymore. Your line lost that right centuries ago. He's mine now to do with as I will."

Alec's father shook his head. "The prerogatives may not be in full force but the obligations are. I'll not give you leave to maim him."

"Then you choose to stand in his place."

"Such is the duty of all leaders."

A ripple ran through the watchers. Those behind Agony leaned forward eager, those behind Alec's father huddled closer together. Alec's father stripped down to the same kind of ha'bit his son would wear a decade and a half later.

"It's not too late, Cyrus. You can still change your mind, still choose the course of reason."

Agony's lips drew back. "You're wrong, Kaleb. There is too much at risk to allow your insolence to go unpunished."

Between one breath and the next Agony exploded into his hybrid shape, and lunged at Alec's dad. For the first time I could actually follow the fight. Agony was smaller and appeared to be weaker but curiously had his opponent on the defensive.

It only took as long as the first few passes for me to figure out why. Both fighters collected a wide array of shallow gashes, but while Agony's quickly began healing, the trickle of blood from Kaleb's didn't slow.

Kaleb was moving around more now, seeking to use his greater reach and speed to create holes in Agony's defense. Agony was fully on the defense now, slowly backing away from Kaleb's blurring strikes.

Agony's retreat took him over rougher ground, and he misstepped slightly. It was a small thing, invisible to most, but it put him just enough off balance to create an opening. Kaleb seized the opportunity, absorbing a deep gash on his right arm as he darted in and clinched.

It wasn't a clean hold. Rather than being completely behind Agony, Kaleb was off to one side. Muscles rippled up and down Kaleb's back as he pulled Agony's arm back, seeking to break the one obstacle preventing him from getting the death hold he was looking for.

Agony's free hand flailed away, cutting long ribbons of blood in Kaleb's right arm and leg. The moonborn on both sides of the fight tensed up as they sensed the critical nature of the next few seconds. Agony's arm was bent back nearly to the breaking point, but blood loss would quickly come into play if Kaleb wasn't able to finish him off.

Even with my enhanced senses I almost missed the turning point. Agony finally got a good grip on Kaleb's leg and started pulling. Kaleb tried to change up his grip, tried for a better hold and Agony slipped away.

Both hybrids renewed their attack but I could feel the initiative slipping back away from Alec's dad. Exhaustion and weakness were robbing him of the advantages he'd been relying on. Agony ducked an overhand slash and scored another set of furrows on Kaleb's ribs.

With a fresh surge of tingling power, Kaleb went back on the offensive, landing three separate blows to Agony's arms. There was no opening this time, but Kaleb lunged forward in a second bid to end the fight. Agony seemed to have been anticipating the move. Rather than backing away, Agony moved into the attack, sticking the talons on his right foot into Kaleb's leg, using it as a platform as he brought his left leg up into Kaleb's chin.

The unimaginable force involved in the blow would've snapped the neck of an elephant but somehow Kaleb rode it out. For a second I thought Kaleb was going to manage to roll away but Agony was already there. Between one heartbeat and the next Agony locked onto Kaleb's back. Once again it wasn't a clean hold but it left one of Agony's hands free to rake his opponent.

My body settled closer to the ground, relaxing like this was a scene I'd seen a hundred times. I saw the same motion repeated over and over as Agony's people came to the conclusion the fight was over.

The blur of motion from the other pack's midst caught everyone by surprise, but the rest of Kaleb's people were only a split second behind.

Donovan hit Agony a split second before Mallory did. Donovan's jaws locked on the back of Agony's throat only to slip off as Mallory knocked Agony off of Kaleb.

My body exploded forward, my perspective shrinking down as I too morphed forms. It was harder to see now. The wolf I'd become focused solely on its next target, gathering its legs underneath it and then launching itself at a brown hybrid.

I sailed past outstretched claws, taking a gash on my right side but I connected with the hybrid's throat, latching on and shaking powerfully. The sensations were almost too much for me. I pulled back, trying to disassociate myself from what I was seeing and feeling. The effort was futile, the experiences kept pulling at me in an emotionless onslaught that refused to be denied.

I caught glimpses of the action in between kills. Mallory fighting Agony as Kaleb struggled to his feet. A group of scared-looking wolves huddled back several yards away from the fighting.

An enemy hybrid sank claws into both my flanks and started ripping at me before a friendly hybrid knocked me free.

I caught more flashes as I flipped through the air. A bloody heap I was sure was Mallory. Kaleb on his knees, Agony tearing at his throat.

I landed and streaked back into the fray. One of Kaleb's wolves intercepted me. We circled for a moment, and then we sprang at each other. As her pulse weakened I caught another glimpse of the combatants.

There was a pool of blood where Mallory had been lying, but her body was gone. The rest of Kaleb's pack had dispersed, leaving Agony's people victorious. My eyes took one last pass across the valley, cataloging corpses and noticing the blood trails indicating where Kaleb's people had fled.

I had a second to wonder at the sheer scope of the violence and then I was back in darkness and the voices were back.

"Much...Later."

I was in a room now: rock walls, empty but for the stone table in the center and the shape shifters watching Agony. I edged slightly closer as if trying to figure out what was on the table but stopped well before I could make sense of the splashes of color.

The longer I stared at the table the more I got the feeling my mind was trying to protect me by refusing to recognize what my eyes were telling me. The object on the table moved and suddenly I found myself staring at Donovan's pain-racked features.

The ghastly sight before me suddenly made sense. I wasn't seeing splashes of color, I was seeing two colors, pale skin and crimson.

After several more seconds I finally pulled myself back far enough to listen to what Agony was saying.

"I do believe you, Donovan. I've believed you for more than an hour now. Mallory died while you were trying to carry her to safety. What you're experiencing now isn't part of the quest for truth. I'm now instructing you regarding the consequences of your actions."

Agony did something to the ruin of Donovan's leg and Donovan screamed.

"You see, I'm very aware that you'll be raising the next generation of Graves children. I want you to think very carefully regarding the course you will lead them on."

The darkness was back. The voices imparted a final set of commands.

"Act...Scared...Say...Nothing."

As soon as the last voice had faded away I found myself back standing against Jasmin's Mercedes. Marco crowed when he saw my eyes flicker back open.

"Bet your tune is going to change now. How does it feel to have a huge hole in your memories?"

I opened my mouth to respond and Oblivion slammed me against the car.

Marco leaned down and whispered into my ear. "How about you and I get a little more friendly? I can show you things Graves hasn't even thought of yet."

My voice came out even and strong. "If you touch me I'll do my absolute best to kill you. I'll probably fail, but you're going to have to kill me to stop me. Trust me, you don't want to be the guy who kills me. Alec will tear you apart regardless of what else it might cost him."

Marco blinked. It wasn't something I saw, more like something I felt. Somehow I knew I'd just made him stop and consider the cost of what he wanted to do. Oblivion had let me go when Marco leaned in. There was nothing stopping me from leaving.

I turned my back on both shape shifters, got into the car and drove away.

Chapter 19

The Jeep was in the driveway when I pulled up to our house. I felt my stomach sink as I realized how mad my mom was going to be. I didn't even have a decent story yet to try and pass off as the truth. The only thing I had going for me was the fact that I'd found a first-aid kit in the car and bandaged myself up in such a way that my sleeve covered everything. It had hurt like crazy when Marco had put his claw into my arm, but it didn't seem as bad now that I'd wrapped it in gauze.

I got ambushed before I was even through the door. Luckily I was able to keep the side of my face that wasn't bruised towards Mom.

"Adriana Paige! Where have you been?"

"Sorry, Mom. I should have left a note but I wasn't thinking."

"A note? Do you have any idea how much trouble you're in? I specifically told you not to go anywhere."

Mom's pacing brought her to the window. Her eyes got really wide when she saw the Mercedes.

"Where did that car come from?"

"It's not what you think, Mom."

"You haven't answered any of my questions yet."

I took a deep breath and hoped whatever was about to come out of my mouth wouldn't have any gaping holes in it.

"When Ben got hurt Jasmin rode in the ambulance with him. Her car's been sitting at the Funcade all night and she was really worried. She asked me to go get it and bring it back here so nothing happened to it."

Mom wasn't stupid, but she normally spent so much time thinking about her art that I could get away with everything short of murder. When that wasn't the case, when she really started focusing on the here and now, it was almost impossible to get anything past her.

"And how did you get to the Funcade to retrieve it for her?"

I could feel the pieces start to unravel. The more truth I used the more believable things tended to be, but I wasn't sure exactly how much truth I could afford to share.

"Ben came and picked me up."

"Ben who was in the hospital getting his leg operated on less than twenty-four hours ago?"

"Um, yeah. I don't think he was supposed to be out yet but he left the hospital anyways."

"Isn't Jasmin interested in Ben?"

"Yeah, that's why we were at the Funcade in the first place."

"Then why didn't Jasmin just ask Ben to get her car?"

"He lives a ways out of town." I was praying that was true. If it wasn't I'd be in even deeper trouble once Mom got to a phone book. "He had a car though so he told her he could come get me and between the two of us we'd take care of things."

"Why exactly couldn't Jasmin get her own car?"

"I'm not sure. It sounded like she was out of town though. She travels some to help Alec with the family business. I'm really sorry, Mom. I should have left a note, or better yet told Jasmin that I couldn't help her until you got back and I could ask permission. I just wasn't thinking."

Mom had been pacing back and forth on the one side of the living room and I'd been very careful to keep the left side of my face out of her line of sight.

She stopped and looked at me for a moment. "Look at me, Adri."

"I am, Mom."

Moving faster than I'd realized she could, Mom reached forward and captured my face between her hands. As her eyes traced the massive bruise Marco had given me, she gasped.

"Adri, what happened?"

I reached out for an explanation but came up blank. "I...I can't tell you."

Mom pulled me towards the couch, more concerned than angry now.

"Sweetie, you need to tell me what happened."

"It's not important. I'm fine."

"It was Alec, wasn't it?"

I felt my mouth drop open that she would even think such a thing. It was pure surprise but she interpreted it as surprise that she'd been right.

I tried to explain. "No!"

"Listen, Adri. I don't care what he's told you, he doesn't love you, especially not since he's doing that to you."

"It's not like that!"

Mom talked right over me. "Boys like Alec can't be trusted. He's got way too much money. It's not healthy for a child to grow up without limits like that. Now he's hitting you. He can't be trusted."

"Mom, Alec didn't hit me."

"I know you're trying to protect him, but he's not worth protecting. You're grounded. I don't want you seeing him anymore."

"He's never hurt me. Why can't you see that?"

"Adri, sweetie, it's not just this. I've started hearing rumors since I got back into town. Why didn't you tell me Brandon and all of his friends had disappeared?"

Somehow I'd never expected my mom to hear the gossip. I'd practiced my story a hundred times in preparation for the police but never expected to need it on my mom.

"They didn't all disappear. Alison, Sam and Jack are all still around. As for why I never told you...I don't know. It just didn't seem that important."

Mom put her head in her hands for a moment. "I really do wish you were caught up stealing cars. That would be better than the truth. I know you're feeling trapped right now, but there's a way out."

"Mom. I'm not trapped. Alec's one of the best guys I've ever met and he hasn't done anything wrong."

"Fine. When you're ready to tell me the truth I'll be here waiting to listen. Until then, you're grounded."

Mom had never stuck with a grounding for more than a few hours. This had already blown the previous record completely out of the water. School was a nightmare. Mom dropped me off in the morning and was there promptly after my shift ended to pick me up.

In between I suffered from a complete lack of social interaction. None of the pack was in school. Neither was Ben or Albert. I sent Alec a text between classes.

Is everything okay? Have news.

Almost two whole hours later Alec finally responded.

Can't really talk. Swing by with news after school?

Grounded. Can't even return Jasmin's car.

She'll be by tomorrow morning.

I broached Jasmin's impending visit on the way home. "Mom, I know I'm grounded, but Jasmin is going to stop by tomorrow morning for her car."

"Back from her trip, huh? Awfully quick even for business, isn't it?"

I didn't bother dignifying the comment with a response. Once we got home I managed to endure Mom's knowing looks for an hour and a half before retreating into my room. All of my usual escapes totally failed me. I finally ended up putting ear buds in and thumbing to a selection of the kind of stuff my mom hated.

The snarling guitars and heavy distortion finally took me away from a world where the boy I loved was in mortal danger and my mom was forbidding me from being there to help. Mom interrupted towards the end of the album to check on me.

I finished the last song and then listened to Mom rattle around the bathroom getting ready for bed. I tried to escape into another album but Mom had ruined the feeling. I was well and truly brought back down to the suckiness of real life.

I sat on the floor for another half an hour and then finally got up to get ready for bed. I had just returned to my room when I heard the light chime of something hitting glass. I ran to my window hoping to see Alec and instead found Ben looking up at me. I shushed him and then crept downstairs. He met me on our porch.

"This totally better be important. I'm already grounded. If my mom catches me down here, I'll be twenty-five before I get out of the house again." My half-serious attempt at humor evaporated away when I saw Ben's face. His eyes were black and bloodshot, like he hadn't slept in days, and his features had taken on a gaunt cast.

"I want to see Jasmin."

"I think she probably wants to see you too, but right now isn't the greatest time."

"You don't understand. I *need* to see her. Tonight."

There was an urgency to his voice that made me uncomfortable.

"I do understand, Ben. You're going through withdrawal, but there isn't anything I can do to help you. Jasmin, Alec, they're all in trouble right now."

"I know. I tried to drive to their place earlier tonight. Two big guys stopped me at the gate. Told me I had to leave."

I seemed to spend all of my time lately trying to figure out how much I could tell someone versus how much I had to lie to them.

"It's okay. If you can just wait a little bit longer those guys will be gone and you and Jasmin can be together."

"Do you really believe that?"

I tried to lie, but nothing would come out. I temporized. "I believe that Jasmin wants to be with you, I just don't know if things are that simple anymore."

"Because I'm addicted to her. She always hated it when I was using. She said when I was high it wasn't really me looking out at her."

I reached over and put a hand on Ben's shoulder. "It doesn't have to be like that. I mean if you can make it a few days, sort of get her out of your system then there won't be anything standing between the two of you."

Ben shook his head violently. "Right, and then what, never touch? You don't understand. I've never had anything hit me like this. She's all I can think about. Those guys. When they touched me, I mean I don't even like guys, but when they touched me it was like I feel when I'm with her."

I moved closer, but Ben shook my hand off. "No. I'm not going to do this. If I'm addicted then I'm addicted, but she can't disappear for days at a time. Stringing me along like that is wrong. The things I'm tempted to do, you don't understand them."

"Jasmin isn't trying to string you along. I can promise you that. She wants to see you again."

Ben looked up at me again and there was a new steel to his gaze. "She has a choice. She can either keep me addicted or she can ignore me. I'm not going through detox twice on this one. She's got twenty-four hours before I leave and never come back."

I tried to talk Ben down, tried to convince him to give Jasmin more time, but it was useless. He was positive he would be through the worst of the withdrawals in the next day or so and didn't want to continue to be tempted.

I even tried to chase him down when he left but I didn't make it very far without shoes. I crept back upstairs about midnight and fell into a fitful sleep.

Mom woke me up the next morning yelling for me to get the door. I stumbled out of bed and found Jasmin and Donovan at the door.

"Oh, right. Sorry guys, I just got up. Let me go get your key, Jas."

"Don't worry about it, I brought a spare and we don't have much time."

I blinked enough of the sleep out of my eyes to finally take in Jasmin's appearance. She looked like she'd been through a war. There were bandages visible peeking out from her clothes in a number of random spots and she had a huge bruise across her face.

Donovan wasn't quite as visibly banged up, but he was moving more stiffly than usual. I wondered if they'd purposefully gone after his good leg. The thought of proper, kind Donovan back on that stone table nearly brought tears to my eyes.

"Are you guys okay? Those weren't Agony's, were they?"

Jasmin tried for nonchalance but couldn't quite pull it off. "No, that's just the natural result of him bringing six other dominants to visit and throwing our power dynamic all to hell. We're pretty much all being treated like submissives right now. The only one they're leaving mostly alone is Alec and they're getting pretty bold even with him lately."

Donovan cleared his throat and Jasmin nodded. "Right, not much time. Have you heard from Ben?"

"How did you know?"

"It was logical. He can't get to me and he trusts you. He's probably associated you with the high too."

"He's not good, Jas. I mean really not good. It looks like he's burning up from the inside out."

Jasmin opened her mouth, looked at Donovan out of the corner of her eye and then shrugged. "I can't do anything about that right now. Alec practically had to throw a hissy fit in order to get the two of us out here to pick up my car. I can't ask him to run those kinds of risks to get me out again. Did Ben seem like he was more or less holding it together? I mean, he wasn't going to go do anything stupid, was he?"

I did feel myself tear up as I recalled the pain in Ben's eyes. "I don't know. He was talking all crazy. He thinks you've addicted him and then hung him out to dry. He doesn't want to go through withdrawal multiple times."

Jasmin reached out and grabbed my arms, almost shaking me. "What exactly did he say?"

"You've got until about midnight tonight. You can either give him another dose or he's going to leave town."

Jasmin's grip tightened as she tried to keep herself under control.

"Jas, you're hurting me."

The words brought forth no response until Donovan reached forward and grabbed her wrist, gradually applying pressure until I could see his knuckles turn white. Jasmin turned on him with a hiss.

For a second I thought she was going to attack but he held his hands up non-threateningly and she visibly brought herself back under control.

"Thanks for letting me know, Adri. Donovan, I'll wait for you at the second to the last turnoff so that we come back together."

Donovan waited until Jasmin's car was backing down the lane before turning back to me. "I'm sorry about that. She's under quite a bit of stress right now."

"No, I understand. Thank you. You...took a risk pulling her off me."

Donovan dismissed the thanks with a wave. "Not such a big risk as you might think. I've helped raise her from the time she was very young. I am submissive to her, but still well-loved by and large."

There was a second where neither of us was quite sure what to say, and then Donovan took a deep breath.

"I'm afraid we really don't have much time. What did Alec's other advisor counsel?"

It took me a second to realize he was talking about Mallory. "She said he should give Agony whatever he wants. Alec needs time for his power to reemerge or to practice with it or whatever."

As Donovan's eyebrows twitched I realized I'd just seen him taken completely off guard for the first time in our acquaintance.

"You didn't know?"

"No, I did not. Alec is wise. No matter how well one bluffs, the task is impossible if those around you tell a different story with their actions. He must play this particular game very close to his chest."

"Is she right? Should Alec really sacrifice whatever it takes to survive Agony's visit?"

Donovan paused for thought. Out of all of the grownups in my life I could always count on him to tell me the truth.

"That is a hard thing. Agony is capable of asking for very dear sacrifices indeed, but I think the advice is correct. If Alec can survive the next few months and truly master his ability he will finally have the strength to put the old order back in place."

I came very close to not telling Donovan about the rest of my trip, but regardless of the risks to Oblivion, or even the risks to me, I couldn't withhold information Alec might need to keep the pack whole.

"I was stopped on the way back. A guy named Marco and Oblivion. They asked me where I'd been. Marco was going to beat it out of me, but Oblivion implied he was going to pull it from my mind."

Donovan's eyes flickered briefly to the fat lip and bruise Marco had left me, but gave no indication of the fear he must feel for the woman he loved.

"When he touched me though, I heard voices. They said if he stole memories it would leave holes. Then he showed me what happened the last time Agony was here. It was like I was there experiencing it for myself but trapped in his body."

Even eighteen hours, later recalling what I'd been shown was almost enough to make me sick. I reached back for the door, leaning against it while I tried to hold myself together.

"I saw the fighting, saw Agony hurt Mallory and kill Alec's dad. It was so terrible."

Donovan helped me over to the porch swing. "It was all a very long time ago. It was terrible, but it's done. Nothing you can do now will change what happened then."

I nodded and brought my breathing back under control. "When it was over he said to act scared and then I was back to myself. They let me go and I came home. I've been running through my memories ever since. I can't think of anything that's missing. I think he was just trying to help. Mallory's safe."

Donovan nodded. "There's never been any indication Oblivion could display memories as well as steal them. This bears some thought. If Oblivion were really ready to make a break from the official line of the Coun'hij it could represent a substantial shift in the balance of power."

After several seconds of silence Donovan shook himself. "Thank you for telling me."

I grabbed Donovan's arm before he could leave. "Do you really think Alec should sacrifice whatever is required in order to keep Agony happy? I saw you on that table. Agony did terrible things to you and never even blinked."

Donovan met my eyes steadily. "Master Alec needs to do whatever is required for him to come into his full power. More is at stake than you realize. My being strapped to that table again is a small price if it saves all of the others Agony would torture otherwise."

Chapter 20

Alec Graves
Graves Estate
Sanctuary, Utah

I was in Donovan's office waiting for him when he and Jasmin got back. It was the one place we were virtually certain had remained locked up the entire time Agony had been here, but even so I didn't fully trust the belief we were safe there. The conversation I'd had with Shawn previously would have created waves between Agony and me if he'd heard it. If what Donovan now knew got out, members of the pack were going to die.

Donovan opened his mouth as if to talk as he came through the door, but I held up my hand. I turned on the white noise generator located next to his desk and then pulled out a sheaf of paper. Using my body and the top sheet of paper I blocked as many sight lines as I could just in case Agony's men had somehow planted some kind of camera in the room.

"The bug sniffers aren't finding anything, but I know Isaac's talked for years about creating a bug that only transmits intermittently maybe coupled with some kind of sensor that tells it when people are in the room."

"Understandable, sir. May I?"

Donovan's generally neat script was hurried and cramped.

A. was successful. M. thinks you should give Agony whatever is needed to survive yourself. We must buy time for your power to reemerge. O. fed A. memories of last visit here. Possibly an ally?

The situation was bleaker knowing that Mallory hadn't been any more able to come up with a brilliant solution than I'd been. I'd expected as much, but still clung to the hope she'd see a way out of the situation that would guarantee everyone both their lives and their self-respect.

I let the top sheet fall back over Donovan's writing and then fed all dozen or so sheets through the shredder at once.

"Do you think she's right, Donovan? Is that really the best option available to us?"

"From a long-term standpoint I think it is. I understand the likely consequences as well as anyone, I think, but I still would urge you to do exactly that."

Donovan reached down and placed his hand on my shoulder in a rare gesture of physical comfort. I looked up to meet his eyes and saw in them an understanding of what it would cost us if Agony decided to force the issue. Donovan had been, to one extent or another, a father to most of the pack.

I couldn't see any way of surviving a fight with Agony's men, not with him and Oblivion thrown in, but the thought of letting one of our friends die still left me feeling sick.

"What about the second piece?"

Donovan considered for several seconds. "I think if it were true it would change everything, but I think it unwise for us to create any plans that include that as a requirement for success."

"You're probably right."

I spared a moment to hope we didn't lose anyone. That would be bad enough all by itself, but losing someone and then finding out later that Oblivion would have backed our play would be even worse.

I stood to leave and then heard something hit the reinforced steel walls of the office hard enough to make the room shake.

I was out into the hall just in time to see Abaddon throw Isaac into the wall again. Isaac shifted into his hybrid form as he rebounded, and turned on his opponent with more fury than I'd seen out of him in years.

The attack caught Abaddon off guard. He was slow changing, which allowed Isaac to get in a solid slash across his chest. Jess was huddled in the corner rocking back and forth as she sobbed quietly.

Abaddon shrugged Isaac off in a complicated move that I'd never seen before. The two hybrids sprang at each other and once again Isaac was the one that went flying. He sailed down the hall, past Jess and nearly hit Jasmin before he managed to get a grip on the floor and bring himself to a stop.

Abaddon rushed past me, knocking Isaac back into the west drawing room. I picked Jess up as I followed along the trail of destruction they'd created. Jasmin joined me just inside the room where we could watch the fight.

"Did you see how it started?"

Jasmin shook her head. "No, but judging by the state Jess is in, Abaddon did something to her or tried to do something. Isaac sprang to her defense and Abaddon started kicking the crap out of him."

Her summation of how Isaac was faring was unfortunately accurate. Abaddon's style of fighting was completely different than anything I'd ever seen before. Rather than trying to get behind Isaac where he could clinch and get a death grip, he kept knocking Isaac away.

Isaac wasn't fighting with his normal calm. Instead he was fighting stupidly. It was every bit as bad as what James usually did, and the result was every bit as bad as I would have expected. Against someone like Vincent, Isaac probably would have already lost the battle for positioning and be seconds from death. Instead he was bleeding from a dozen different places to Abaddon's two and maybe a minute from losing the fight.

There was a desperation to the fight now as Isaac sensed it resolving in Abaddon's favor. Isaac charged again, getting his talons into Abaddon's right leg before being driven back with a flurry of slashes.

Jasmin crowded in close to my side. "Shouldn't we do something? I mean it's three to one. We could easily kill Abaddon and shift the balance of power in our favor."

I shook my head. That was exactly the kind of thing that Agony was looking for. "It's a dominance fight. They have to work out who's dominant to who."

Jasmin looked like she was going to argue with me but Donovan shook his head at her. I turned back to the fight as another crash announced the destruction of more furniture. Isaac was on the ground now, struggling to get up as Abaddon glided forward.

I moved between them, but mostly faced Isaac. "You're beaten. He's dominant to you and you're going to have to just deal with it."

Isaac shook his head. "Jess. I have to protect her."

"No, you've just proved you can't protect either of you. Stand down."

He wasn't going to listen. I could see it in his eyes, so I did the only thing I could to keep him alive. I stomped down on his arm nearly hard enough to break bone as I let the hands holding Jess turn into nightmarish things that were topped by the same kind of semi-retractable claws he and Abaddon were already sporting. I didn't have to actually say anything, the threat was clear.

I turned to Abaddon. "There's no need for the fight to continue. You've proven you're dominant to him, killing him would be a waste."

"It's my decision, my right." Abaddon's voice came out deeper than normal, but there was an edge to it that couldn't be explained just by the different physiology between human and hybrid forms. He longed for the kill.

"He's your second and he wasn't any kind of challenge. Maybe I shouldn't stop with him."

My beast surged forward, filling the room with a level of power that made the fireworks that had accompanied their fight look like sparklers. As powerful as Agony and the rest of the Coun'hij ultimately were, it was the sick pieces of work like Abaddon and Marco who ultimately made it possible for such a small group to hold an entire race hostage.

The entire Coun'hij would have been swarmed under decades ago if not for the fact that they'd drawn together so many like-minded hybrids who lived for the sadistic thrill of seeing the rest of us brought low.

It was all I could do to stop myself from springing at Abaddon. My beast had largely been quiet for the last few weeks. Even the fight with Vincent hadn't really drawn it to the surface like this. Somewhere along the way it had gained power, had eroded more of that slim margin of willpower I used to keep it leashed.

I was so busy trying to master myself that it took me a minute to realize Abaddon had actually backed up a step. I stalked forward, just enough to make him nervous without actually getting close enough to make him attack me.

"If you attack me it will be the last thing you ever do. The same tradition that gives you the right to kill Isaac right now would finally give me the pretext I need to end you."

I loosened my grip on my beast just the slightest bit and felt my eyes bleed over to a lighter blue as the power level impossibly ratcheted up even more. I could almost see Abaddon's thoughts. He'd been told to create incidents, to tear at the bonds holding our pack together. He'd been prepared to do that, eager even after my fight with Vincent had made him think stories about my power were so much hot air.

Faced with the very real possibility that I'd just been holding back for some incomprehensible reason, Abaddon wasn't so eager anymore. He'd already lost a certain amount of status when Isaac had attacked him rather than bowing down before his towering reputation. He could regain it if he pushed me into a fight and then killed me, but he'd never felt that kind of power out of a single individual before.

Abaddon backed slowly away and then disappeared around a corner. I set Jess down next to Isaac and then left the room. I could feel Isaac's eyes follow me out of sight. I didn't need to look back to know they were filled with hate. We'd stood together against Brandon's overwhelming numbers, against James' craziness, and never flinched, but I'd just burned that history up like cobwebs. It remained to see whether or not any loyalty would survive the next few days, but I'd had no other choice. This at least gave him and Jess both a chance to see tomorrow.

Chapter 21

Mom and I had the biggest fight ever once Donovan left. Apparently she'd been watching from the upstairs window. Seeing Jasmin leave all banged up and Donovan limp away after talking to me alone had apparently been the last straw.

"You're not to talk to Alec or any of his friends ever again. I don't even want you associating with them at school."

"That's not fair. None of us have done anything wrong!"

"No, you've done plenty wrong, you're just not admitting to the rest of it."

"If Dad were here he'd be reasonable."

Mom's eyes blazed at my unfair jab. "Yes, please remind me of what I've lost. You're so busy wallowing in your self-pity you never bother to think about the fact that this is hard on me too."

"Right, because it was my choice to uproot you and drag you halfway across the country."

"I did what I had to do to take care of us."

I nearly turned and walked away. It would have been the smart thing. I would have gotten in trouble but nothing compared to what came next.

"No, you did what you've done so you could go play photographer. I haven't done anything wrong, but it would serve you right if I had. You spend most of your time out in the mountains expecting me to raise myself. Well, guess what. I did and now you've got to deal with the fact that I'm an adult too and you've been away too much to have any idea what I do with my time. Dad would roll in his grave if he could see you now."

Mom slapped me. Not like Marco had slapped me, lazy and secure in his own power. Mom hauled back and hit me with everything she had. I ran upstairs and locked my bedroom door.

I guess it was a moral victory. I'd pushed her so far she'd done something she regretted. It didn't feel like I'd won, it felt like my world was coming to an end.

Mom came by half an hour later and tried to apologize through the door. I put my head under the pillow and ignored her. Eventually she walked away and I quietly cried myself to sleep. We'd finally crossed a line. There'd been plenty of tension and resentment between us before but we'd buried it deep enough that neither had really realized it was there. Instead we had tried to pull together to make our life without Dad and Cindi work.

I didn't see us ever going back to that semi-happy state of affairs. Every time we looked at each other we'd think about the things that'd been said. We'd been mad, but mad sometimes just meant you were actually honest for a change.

I tried to lose myself in music again, tried books, homework. Nothing worked. I settled into a kind of funk where nothing mattered. It wasn't a panic attack, but it had some of the same overtones as how I felt when I woke up afterwards.

I heard Mom come back and try to talk to me again, but the knowledge didn't manage to pierce the comfortable numbness that surrounded me. Even when she got frustrated and yelled through the door it didn't manage to move me. Her words slid around the edge of my protection and then slipped away.

Eventually darkness came bringing with it extra insulation from the world. I don't know how long my phone rang before it finally pierced the numbness. I finally looked down and saw Alec's name on the caller ID.

"Adri, where have you been?"

"Home. Here in my room."

"I'm sorry, but I need you here. Agony's demanded your presence again."

I tried to focus. It was Alec, he was important and I needed to be there for him, but the words were so far away and my mind was so lethargic.

"I'm grounded. Mom thinks you killed Brandon and that I'm involved."

There was a pause as Alec processed what I'd just said and how I was responding.

"How much trouble are you in?"

"Lots. We had a really big fight."

Thinking started getting easier again. Thinking about the yelling match hurt, but it was waking my faculties back up.

"I wish I didn't have to ask this of you. I wouldn't ask if there wasn't so much riding on it. Can you sneak out?"

"I think Mom's gone. Getting out won't be the problem, getting back in will be though. She's the maddest I've ever seen her."

"Okay, I need you to sneak out. A couple of Agony's men will meet you on the road, start into town and they'll pick you up on the way."

"What's going on?"

"I wish I could say for sure. All I know is we've got to be getting close to seeing the big finish."

"All right. I'll leave in the next couple of minutes."

"Before you go, there's a small package in the bottom of your dresser. I hope you won't need it, but you'd better bring it just in case."

My legs were weak and shaky from sitting in one position for so long. I stumbled over to my dresser and found Alec's mystery package. It turned out to be a long, knife. I gingerly pulled it out of the sheath. It looked wickedly sharp and gave me a sick feeling in the pit of my stomach. If things were bad enough that I'd need a knife to protect myself then I was already in over my head. I had no idea how to use a knife.

I slid the knife back into its sheath and noticed the clever clip that would attach it to a belt. I stood there for a minute or so debating before pulling on some jeans and hooking the knife onto them so it was hidden under my tank top.

I crept out of my room, verified the Jeep was really gone, and then started hiking down the lane. Agony's guys found me before I'd gone more than a hundred yards or so. They pulled up in a large, black SUV.

I didn't recognize the guy driving it, but Oblivion opened the door and motioned me in. The driver wasn't chatty and Oblivion was his normal terse self so we passed the ten-minute trip in silence.

When we arrived, Oblivion escorted me into the house while the other guy parked the vehicle. It felt wrong to be in Graves manor without having been greeted at the door by Donovan. I was about to ask Oblivion where we were headed when I heard Rachel's screams.

I reacted without thinking, running towards the sound. I kept expecting Oblivion to pull me up short. He was obviously faster than me, but somehow I made it to the door to Alec's mom's suite without him catching me.

The main room had been transformed from the airy, sunny haven to a place of nightmare. Rachel was the one screaming, but it was her mom who was being hurt. Only hurt wasn't quite the word.

Marco had tied both of them up and was slowly rubbing his hand along Mrs. Graves' face. The contact was drawing little tremors of pleasure from its target, but Rachel was screaming and straining at her bonds.

"Stop it. Don't do that to her, it's not right."

Rachel's mom opened her eyes long enough to look at her daughter. "Shut up. It's what I've wanted all these years."

"That's right, Samantha. All these years missing the touch of a real man."

Marco returned his hand to her cheek and smiled coldly as her eyes rolled back up inside her head.

"She's an addict. You're violating every law regarding the Ja'tell bond. She can't decide for herself."

"I won't violate any laws. I'll take her with me when I leave. She's still a handsome woman and I rather expect that Alec will loosen the famous Graves purse strings to make sure she's taken care of appropriately. She'll never even look back, never miss you guys."

Rachel had already been through so much. I'd been there when she'd cried herself to sleep because her mother was so far gone she didn't recognize her own daughter. I couldn't let her lose what little bit of her mom she had left.

I stepped forward, moving closer to Marco as my hand slipped underneath my shirt. I didn't know the first thing about fighting, but I wasn't thinking, I just unsheathed the knife and stabbed.

Marco was completely surprised. I managed to stab him a second time before he backhanded me into the wall. A collection of plants in wrought-iron stands more or less broke my fall. Somehow I'd managed to keep a hold of the knife. I rolled back to my feet just in time to see Marco explode into his hybrid shape.

I felt my mouth go dry but I dropped down into a crouch, trying to drop my center of gravity so I could move in whatever direction I needed to. Rachel screamed, and then suddenly Oblivion was between Marco and me, shaking his head at the hulking enforcer.

It wasn't possible that Oblivion was actively going to defend me. He had to have known what was going on here. If he wasn't going to defend me though maybe he was willing to buy me some time. Somehow I kept the fear at bay enough to think.

"Rachel. Rachel!"

I'd never yelled at Rachel, she'd always seemed too delicate to survive anything more than a stern look. I knew that wasn't true though and I needed her knowledge of shape shifter rules and tradition. Somehow the scream managed to miraculously get through to her. I saw her eyes track over to me and her breathing steady.

"I need you to think about this situation. Is there any reason why Marco wouldn't want to kill me for what I've just done?"

"He...he's just lost a lot of status. You hurt him, forced him to shift shapes, so his body is back to a blank canvas. One of the traditional ways to mitigate the damage would be to kill you."

Marco was scared of Oblivion, scared of the possibility of losing everything he was when the memories were sucked out of him. Even so, I could see him working up to an attack.

"You can do this, Rach. There's got to be something."

"Alec. It's Alec. We're all under his protection. If Marco kills you, then Alec would be within his rights to challenge Marco. Alec would kill him and then Agony would be down a fighter. It's the kind of provocation that the Coun'hij usually uses as an excuse themselves."

Marco growled. His voice was deeper now than when he was in his human form. "I can always say your attack on me was unprovoked. I kill all three of you and there's nobody left to dispute my version of the truth."

I felt a calm certainty flow through me at Rachel's words. "No. Or rather you could do that, but it won't stop Alec from killing you and you know it. If you kill all three of us, the three most important people in his life, then nothing will stop him from killing you in turn."

Marco shifted back and forth, as if trying to decide how to get around Oblivion. "No guarantee that he can take me. Besides it would then provide Agony with exactly the excuse he needs. We'll rip your pack apart and salt the ground. Agony will finally get to finish the job he started with Graves' old man."

I wiped the dagger, dripping with Marco's blood, on my leg. "Trust me. Alec would destroy you. Are you really ready to die for Agony? Agony's not even willing to face Alec himself. This whole visit is nothing more than an attempt to maintain appearances. You all know what Alec is capable of. If Agony backs him into a corner your entire group will die."

Marco's head tilted to the side, considering my words as his nostrils flared in an attempt to smell whether or not I was telling the truth. I was betting all our lives on me being too far gone in shock for the normal signals to work.

The stalemate held for several seconds before Marco turned away. He threw a nearby chair through the lovely full-length windows as he left, but he left. Oblivion backed several steps away and then watched me as I cut both Rachel and her mom free.

Rachel's mom weakly pushed us away, a faint mewing sound coming from the back of her throat, but she was too frail to stop us. I sheathed my knife and then we half carried her out of the room.

As we turned onto the main hall I realized I was shaking, and a second later the tremble got too bad for me to keep moving. I set Mrs. Graves' feet down and wrapped my arms around myself, trying to hold things together long enough for the adrenaline to finish flushing out of my system.

Rachel's mom curled up against the wall as soon as Rachel put her down, and suddenly Rachel's arms were around me.

"Rach, why am I even here?"

"It's standard procedure. The Coun'hij always wants as many non-combatants around as possible. It's leverage against the rest of the pack actually standing up to them. Alec knew this might happen, it's why he's been so careful to try and keep you ignorant of everything. As long as you didn't know too many of our secrets, there was a possibility that whoever the Coun'hij sent would decide not to suck you further into our world. It's not like there's not already plenty of us who can't defend ourselves here. One more human shield more or less shouldn't have made a difference."

The last sentence had more defiance to it than I'd ever heard from Rachel. I looked up, half afraid that Oblivion would be angry, but he seemed unaffected by the heat in her voice.

I grabbed Rachel's arm, willing her not to say something that would make our situation worse, and took a deep breath.

"We'd better get moving again, Rach. I don't want to make things worse for Alec and the others."

All too soon we found ourselves back in the underground cavern where Alec had fought Vincent. The torches were back, barely managing to illuminate the gathered groups of shape shifters. With our arrival the entire pack was here. Alec sported a number of ugly-looking gashes on his arms, but he looked to be in the best shape of any of our shape shifters. I'd already had a chance to catalog most of Jasmin and Donovan's wounds. James and Dominic stood close together, him favoring his right leg, her with nasty bruises ruining the perfection of her otherwise flawless dark skin.

Isaac's ha'bit had been ripped away from his chest to show a peculiar pattern of wounds that made it look as though someone had tried to tear out his heart. James had looked angry, but I'd gotten so used to that expression on his face that it hadn't made me think twice. The same expression now graced Isaac's face and the loss of his trademark calm was one more clue as to just how bad things had been.

Jess looked like she wanted to fold in on herself. Her right arm was a mess of bandages, most of which were stained crimson from their futile attempt to stop the bleeding. She'd taken far more than her share of mental and emotional scars in the fight with Brandon. We'd never particularly been close, but I hurt for her at the thought of what this week must have done to her.

As we crossed the last little distance to our pack, I looked the rest of them over one by one. It was more and more of the same. Even those who'd already been maimed by Agony on his last visit bore fresh signs of abuse. Donovan, Andrew, Addison, everyone.

Donovan took Rachel's mom from us, careful to keep from touching her bare skin. As he laid her down in the back of our group I took in the other side of the cavern. I'd somehow expected to find Agony's men more or less unmarred. I hadn't expected to find them sporting at least one respectable wound each, nor had I expected to find them missing their piercings and tattoos.

Some of them had replicated a smattering of their earlier piercings, but of the whole group, only Oblivion still had his tattoos. I didn't know if Agony had a dedicated group of enforcers who accompanied him on every visit, or if he drew from a larger pool used by the Coun'hij as a whole, but either way these men had lost their cool. Our people had proved that the Coun'hij's men weren't untouchable and managed to do it without crossing that treacherous line that would have let Agony wipe us all out.

It couldn't help but make it that much harder the next time Agony needed bully boys to go terrorize somebody. Alec had somehow guided our people in a kind of guerrilla warfare that had chipped at the enforcers' composure and cohesion. He'd eaten away at them from the inside out. The only question remained what the ultimate price would be. Our people had been too abused to easily forget what they'd been through, and I found myself wondering just how much of his precious store of goodwill Alec had used up.

Agony looked up from his conversation with Marco and shook his head. "Young Graves, your pet human has been free with her promises of your vengeance. I'm quite curious, would you really have killed Marco if she'd been killed for interfering where she had no business?"

Alec's answer came without hesitation. "If Adri felt she needed to interfere with whatever Marco was doing then I have every faith that she was in fact doing exactly what needed doing. In those circumstances I would have indeed killed Marco for harming her. I will always extract vengeance for harm against those of my pack who are loyal to me."

"You are wise to make such a promise only regarding the loyal members of your pack. It has come to my attention that not all members of your pack are as loyal as you might wish."

This was the big surprise. I could feel it and apparently everyone else could feel it too. Agony's people moved a step or two forward, crowding us. That didn't surprise me as much as our response. I got a quick response to my earlier question regarding how much damage Agony had done to our unity. Rather than the entire pack clustering more tightly together, the hybrids on the front and to the outside, we shifted slightly further apart. Instead of a circular group we were a long, irregular line.

Isaac moved closer to Jess and James moved closer to Dominic. Jasmin settled back to where she was nearly touching Rachel and the three newest members all huddled together. Of the entire pack, only Alec and Donovan didn't move from their places. They remained motionless and the pack moved away.

"I assure you that any possible disloyalty will be dealt with appropriately as a purely internal matter."

Agony shook his head slowly back and forth. "I wish it were as simple as that. Members of your pack have been passing privileged information to an outsider for quite some time."

The words made me think back to Mallory's statement that but for the fact Vincent was with

Agony, she would have bet on there being a spy in our midst.

"While I would in any circumstance mourn for the resources this individual has no doubt drained from the pack, this betrayal is made worse by the identity of the individual to whom the betrayal was made. I've only just learned today that these individuals collectively planned on breaking off to form their own pack and then launching a complicated plot to topple the Coun'hij from our rightful place of authority."

I knew Agony was lying. I figured it must be even more infuriating for the shape shifters in our pack who could tell for sure that nothing being said was true. I spared a glance at Alec to see how he was responding, but he hadn't moved a muscle since Agony had started his speech.

"If this had happened, untold turmoil would have gripped the world. There would have been no group prepared and able to deal with the myriad threats lurking on the periphery of human society. The weres would have run wild, their population exploding in a way it hasn't for centuries. Worse, the blood drinkers would have likely become aware of our existence and we would in turn have been hunted down by yet another foe whose numbers aren't constrained by paltry things like birthrates."

I started to turn towards Jasmin, hoping for a clue regarding what Agony was referring to. I nearly missed the attack. Agony's men had continued to slowly drift forward as he'd talked. Our backs had been against the wall already. There wasn't anywhere for us to go but closer together, the hybrids crowding around Alec now that the threat was upon them.

Vincent had positioned himself directly before Alec, slightly in front of Agony. It was an optimal position for guaranteeing Vincent a rematch with Alec.

Agony finished speaking, stepped forward as he morphed shapes, and then fastened his claws on Vincent's unprotected human neck. At the same time Abaddon sprang forward and ripped Alison away from Jack and Sam.

I stumbled back into Donovan, my mind reeling, and saw Isaac on the ground, knocked down by Oblivion who had Jess's still form in his arms, hands pressed against her head as if preparing to crush it.

Alec moved in a blur, not towards Agony as I'd expected, but towards Isaac, knocking Isaac to the ground again as he tried to roll back to his feet. "Hold!"

A yelp of pain and a sickening crunch hauled me around to see Jack and Sam ignore Alec's command. The two transformed into wolves and launched themselves at Abaddon in a blur but Marco and another hybrid were ready.

The fight was longer than I'd expected, but still brief and bloody. Abaddon and the others left Alison, Sam and Jack on the ground, bloody heaps that would never breathe again. Alec spent the entire fight with his foot on Isaac's throat while the rest of the pack sat in stunned silence.

Agony stood motionless for several seconds, possibly waiting to see if anyone else would throw themselves at his men.

"I apologize for the manner in which the announcement had to be made, but you've been cleansed of the traitor."

Alec was shaking now, but his foot was still on Isaac's throat, his hand still motioned the rest of us back. "I ask that your man unhand Jessica and return her to us. He's no doubt drained her mind. As such, she's no longer a traitor."

Agony didn't like that. Even I could tell that he'd expected Oblivion to kill her, but apparently he wasn't able to dispute Jess's newfound innocence.

"We'll take our leave of you now."

At a gesture from Agony, Oblivion released Jess and then the other group backed away from us and out of the cavern. Dom, Jasmin and Rachel all rushed over to Jess' nearly still form while Donovan set Alec's mother down and hurried over to check Alison's body.

I meant to help, either with Jess or with the others, but my body refused to function. Instead I numbly watched as Donovan gently closed Alison's eyes and moved on to the other two.

There was a ripping sound and then suddenly a heavily scarred wolf crouched among the remnants of Andrew's wheelchair. The old shape shifter launched himself at Alec with a growl of hatred but his injuries robbed him of the speed and power he'd have needed to have any chance. The attack was so slow that even I saw it coming. Alec reached out and caught Andrew by the throat, never even shifting forms as he slammed the old wolf into the ground.

Isaac tried to use the distraction to fight free, but Alec somehow spun him around in a blur of motion. When the trio stopped moving Alec's left hand had transformed to the deadly claws of his hybrid form, all of which were wrapped around Isaac's human throat.

"If you transform I will kill you. Jess isn't dead. The experiences are gone but she's still here and she'll need both of you to deal with what's happened to her. I want your word, each of you that you'll commit no act of vengeance, not against me or the Coun'hij, without my permission. I can't have you wasting yourselves in a futile attempt at balancing the scales."

First Andrew and then Isaac nodded their agreement. Alec released both of them. "Jas, Isaac, James and Dom. We all need to be upstairs. There's always a chance that Agony's men will decide to come back and clean house if we don't make a good show of force. The rest of you follow as you're able, but don't get between the fighters."

Alec and the others swept up the stairs. I looked blankly at Rachel for several seconds before shuffling over to Jess. She had started waking up.

"What...I mean, who are you and where am I?"

Suddenly I wished that I'd opted to help with Rachel's mom or one of the others. I was the last person who should be trying to explain things to Jessica. I barely knew myself what was going on.

"My name is Adri. I'm afraid that right now you probably won't remember anything, but you're safe."

Jess nodded and leaned up against me. It reminded me of the time I'd gone to a friend's house and her niece had visited. The little girl had run to her aunt, curled up on her lap and promptly gone to sleep.

"Do you remember your name?"

"No. That's odd isn't it? I mean shouldn't I remember it?"

I shook my head. "No, actually I expected that you wouldn't remember. It's Jess. Jessica actually, but your friends all call you Jess."

"Friends...they are important. I'm glad I have some. Do I have many? Are we friends?"

"You have a few friends, but the important thing isn't the number, it's how loyal your friends are, and you've got some very loyal friends."

Jess nodded happily and then looked over at the others. "Are those some of my friends? Are they okay? It looks like some of them are hurt."

"They will be okay, but if you feel up to it we should go help them. If you want to take my hand I'll help you up, but be very careful, you're quite strong."

That earned me a smile. "I think I'd like to be strong. Maybe someday I can be as pretty as you too."

We stopped in front of Andrew. He was doing his best to control his emotions, but hadn't been able to slow the tears that had started as soon as he'd resumed his human form.

"You feel familiar. Do we know each other?"

Andrew looked up at me with pleading eyes, apparently unable to bring himself to respond. I cleared my throat and moved Jessica's hand down to his arm.

"This is Andrew. You knew each other very well and are very important to each other."

"Like family?"

"Yes, like family."

As we were carrying Andrew towards the stairs Jess looked over at me. "How did my memories get lost?"

"A bad man stole them from you."

"Were my friends not around to stop him?"

I felt my throat tighten up and tears start to gather at the corners of my eyes. "No, sweetie, we were all here."

"Then why didn't you all stop him?"

"I don't know."

Chapter 22

Alec made sure that Agony and his men were well on their way and then he and the others came back. I'd just finished helping get Andrew and Jess settled in their rooms when Alec found me.

"I'm glad I caught you alone, Adri. We need to talk."

I pushed past him. "I don't want to talk to you right now."

Alec grabbed my arm, not holding hard enough to hurt me, but hard enough I couldn't escape. "I know you're mad right now. I didn't want you to see something like that. I've been working from the first day to try and guarantee that you wouldn't get involved in the infighting with the Coun'hij."

"Well, it's good to know this wasn't just a one-off, unexpected kind of thing. Apparently you were always capable of this kind of thing."

"That's not fair."

"You want to talk about fair? Let's talk about Alison and Jess. Neither of them were passing information to Vincent and you know it."

Alec let go of me and ran his hand through his hair. "You're right. Neither of them did anything to deserve what they got. Unfortunately what happened to them wouldn't have been changed by anything we could have done. Alison was dead before any of the rest of us could even move."

"Alison wasn't the only one who died today."

"What? Vincent?"

I'd thought I was mad, but the thought of Alec thinking of a piece of slime before he'd think of Jack or Sam stoked my fury to a raging bonfire. "No, not Vincent. Sam and Jack died trying to protect Alison and you never lifted a finger. They were part of your pack. They trusted you, depended on you, and you just let them throw their lives away."

"I couldn't stop them. I was only barely able to stop Isaac. They chose to attack Abaddon. I didn't force them to do it."

"You could have attacked. They were down a hybrid and there was a chance that Oblivion would have helped or at least stepped aside."

Alec shook his head. "We would have lost. My power isn't working anymore and Oblivion wouldn't have stepped aside. Jess losing her memories told us that. He would have fought at Agony's side and the entire pack would have been destroyed. I had to choose between Isaac or the other two and I chose to save Isaac."

"You didn't choose Isaac, you decided against Jack and Sam. You've never valued them. They've been second-class citizens since the day they joined the pack. You should have just killed them when you killed the rest of Brandon's pack."

Alec's eyes had changed. They'd started taking on the light blue of his beast, which was never a good sign. Usually I didn't worry because I knew he wouldn't hurt me. Now I was just too mad to stop and think of the implications.

"I chose Isaac because he stood by me for years when those other three were helping Brandon try to kill us all. I chose Isaac because Jess is going to need him over the next few months or years as she tries to forge a new identity. And yes, I chose Isaac because he's more of an asset to the pack than Sam and Jack put together. That's the piece that really bothers you, isn't it?"

"They shouldn't be second-class citizens because they can't kill as well as Isaac. That's exactly the kind of crap Brandon would have said."

Alec picked up a shake as he moved towards me. "I hate to break it to you, but that's the way the real world works. We aren't civilized. It's all we can do sometimes to keep our beasts in check, and how well you fight, how well you can kill has a direct impact on whether or not the pack survives to see another day. If you scratch away the veneer of civilization out there you'll find out it's exactly the same, you've just had too much of a sheltered, perfect life to realize it."

I wished that Alec had just hit me instead. For him, of all people, to discount what I'd been through was an almost physical pain. I lashed out with the only thing I could think of that had any chance of causing him the same kind of hurt.

"I've been wrong all this time. You really are nothing more than an animal."

I turned and walked away, ignoring his sudden intake of breath. I made it all the way to the front door before I heard him following.

"Where are you going?"

"I'm going home. I've got a spectacular fight waiting for me."

"You're going to have to wait a few more minutes. I need half an hour or so to check on the pack. Things are really strained right now and…"

I cut him off. "I don't want a ride home from you. I'll walk."

"Don't be ridiculous. It will take you hours to walk home, and it's not safe. There's still a chance that Agony's guys are in the area."

"I'm not safe here, not really. I'll take my chances on the road."

I could hear Alec's teeth grinding and his knuckles went white on the doorknob. "If you'll wait five minutes I'll get Rachel to give you a ride home."

I turned on Alec, poking him as hard in the chest as I was able. "How dare you bully Rachel after everything she's gone through this week. If you force her to come up here and drive me home I swear I'll never talk to you again."

Alec pulled his keys out and dropped them at my feet. "Take the Porsche. Leave it in your driveway, or in the trees a mile or so past your lane. I'll come get it in a day or two when I'm able."

Mom was waiting for me when I pulled up in Alec's Porsche. I'd considered leaving it on the road. I was pretty sure it was just going to give Mom one more thing to freak out about, but I didn't want to spend the next two days worrying that it'd been stolen.

As I came through the door Mom grabbed me by the shoulders and shook me. "What the hell were you thinking? I was about thirty seconds from calling the cops."

"I'm sorry, Mom. Something came up. Rachel needed me."

"You mean Alec needed you."

"The whole family needed me."

Mom let me go and started pacing back and forth across the living room floor. "Adri, real friends don't ask you to do things that will get you in trouble. I like Rachel, but can you honestly tell me that you didn't see or do anything tonight that made you feel uncomfortable?"

I felt myself flinch. I knew it was a lost cause, but I lied anyways. "Mom, nothing happened tonight."

"I don't believe you. Even if you're telling the truth, it's only a matter of nothing happened yet. I'm telling you, Alec is not the good guy you think he is."

After everything I'd just seen, everything that had just happened, it felt odd to defend Alec. "He's a good guy; he's just caught in a tough situation right now."

"No, Adri. That's not how it works. Tough times don't hide a person's true nature; trials bring that true nature out. The things you're seeing now are things that have always been there in Alec, he's just been hiding them."

I shook my head. "I can't believe that. He's just been forced off to a path other than what he would have chosen for himself. He's a good person who really does care about others."

"Then your only hope of saving him is to give him the kind of massive wakeup call that will knock him back onto the right path."

I felt tears start to fill my eyes. I opened my mouth to respond but she talked right over me.

"You're not mature enough to make this kind of decision, so I'm making it for you. There will be no more Alec, no more Rachel, no more of any of that. This whole episode of your life is over."

Chapter 23

It was an unseasonably warm day. Nothing compared to the temperatures when we'd first arrived in Sanctuary, but it reminded me somehow of the furnace that had greeted us when we got out of the moving truck so long ago. Minnesota would have snow by now.

Mom pulled the Jeep over to the side of the road. We'd had another fight. She'd wanted to drive me right up to the door, but I'd finally managed to win some privacy. Odd to think after I'd fought so hard that I now didn't want to make the trip alone.

I sat fingering what was left of the necklace Alec had given me for several seconds before Mom cleared her throat. "I really am sorry about your necklace, Adri."

"It's okay, it was an accident. It was bound to happen-glass is only about the most breakable substance known to man."

"Still, I feel bad. I never would have guessed that it would splinter like that."

It was an odd break. The glass hadn't shattered or even simply broken in half like I would have expected when Mom knocked it off the coffee table. Instead a long sliver of glass had separated from the main heart. I'd kicked possible causes around off and on for most of a day now. All I could come up with was that there must have been some kind of flaw accidentally built into the piece.

"I'll bet we can find a way to fix it still, dear."

"No. You can't glue glass together. Even if you could, it wouldn't really be fixed, it would be ugly."

I angled the heart back and forth, watching the way it caught the light, throwing off small rainbows of light. In some ways what it had lost in perfection of form had been partially made up for by the way light now refracted through it.

I knew better, but still couldn't help myself. My thumb slid forward to the broken edge. It was the lightest of touches but that was all the razor edge of the glass required to slice into my skin. I was wrong, it wasn't still pretty.

"It can't be put together and it's dangerous now. Neither piece will ever really be safe again."

I exited the Jeep before Mom could respond, and started up the asphalt lane. I'd been to Alec's so many times, but usually in too much of a hurry to appreciate the scenery. Andrew and Donovan really did do an amazing job maintaining the grounds.

I rang the doorbell, managing a tentative smile for Donovan. "Mistress Paige. I'm glad to see you're okay. I've spent no small amount of time worrying about how you've held up after the events of this last week."

"I'm okay, Donovan. You're doing okay too?"

"I'm recovering apace. None of my injuries were inflicted by Agony so I expect to be as fit as ever shortly. Are you not coming in?"

I shook my head. "I don't have long." I opened my mouth to ask to see Alec, but something made me pause. I knew that Donovan's loyalty to Alec and Rachel was absolute, but I still somehow trusted him to tell me the truth.

"Donovan, Agony was lying, right?"

I'd never really seen Donovan at a loss for words, but it took him several seconds to respond.

"To be honest, Miss Adri, I'm not really sure. I'm sure it seems like our ability to decipher between honesty and falsehood is nearly magical, but in fact it's more along the lines of an educated guess backed up by more observational data than you have access to."

My frustration with the answer was probably woefully apparent to him. After another several seconds he sighed and then continued.

"Our ability to detect lies breaks down the worst when dealing with one of our own kind.

Agony is quite good at suppressing his body's natural tells. Almost too good. Actually, his ability in that area borders on what you'd see from a psychopath. When you add in that he's quite good at mixing truth and lies together, it becomes very difficult to hazard a guess as to whether or not he was lying."

I shook my head, anger starting to chip away at the respect I usually showed the old butler.

"It's obvious he lied. I don't believe Jess was working with Vincent. Even if you believe she was capable of turning against Isaac and the rest of the pack, you have to know that she'd never have chosen to work with Vincent."

Donovan nodded. "Indeed, I don't believe Jess did the things that Agony said she did, but I don't believe everything he said was a lie. That doesn't...feel...right against what I observed that night."

"So what, Alison was in league with Vincent?"

I was really trying to keep the hostility out of my voice, but even I could tell that I wasn't doing a very good job. Donovan didn't seem rattled though.

"No, I don't think Alison was ambitious enough to throw her lot in with Vincent."

"You're contradicting yourself, Donovan. Either there was truth to what Agony said or there wasn't. You can't have it both ways."

"Jack possibly, he was stupid enough, but my money would have been on Sam. He was ambitious enough for a wolf with several times his ability. He knew Vincent, and I think he was higher up in Brandon's pack than anyone ever let on."

I shook my head, trying to deny Donovan's words, but he talked right over me for the first time that I could remember.

"I think that Sam was working with Vincent, not to rise up against the Coun'hij, but to give Agony and Vincent an inside track in their efforts to rip this pack apart. Agony always likes a sure thing and by all accounts he should have succeeded. I doubt you'll ever really understand how close he came to obtaining his goal, but when Alec managed to steer us more or less unscathed to that last meeting Agony needed a win of some kind."

Donovan looked off into the distance for a moment. "The Coun'hij rules through fear and fear alone. Any real uprising among the packs could bring them down. It would probably be bloody, but it's a very real possibility, one which Agony understands extremely well. Each and every one of his actions has to be couched in a way that provides at least some justification, or he could push the rest of my kind over the edge into rebellion. At the same time, the Coun'hij can't afford to ever come away second best in a confrontation or they risk that the fear that they depend on to keep control will start to erode away out from under them. Agony couldn't leave without killing one or more members of our pack, not if he wanted to stop Alec from becoming a rallying point."

I could follow the logic. That didn't mean Donovan was right, but it made a kind of sick sense. Vincent had been helping Agony, but killing one of his own helped sell the legitimacy of Agony's story. Vincent was the newest of the Coun'hij's thugs, so it probably hadn't bothered Agony's other guys in the slightest. Killing Sam would have been more believable, but nobody outside of our pack would have known the difference. By attacking Alison it had been practically guaranteed that Sam would jump into the fray, and where Sam went Jack usually followed. If Isaac had been the slightest bit faster, half of the pack would have been sucked into a fight with Agony's men and summarily killed.

Donovan looked me in the eyes for several heartbeats and then shook his head. "Agony wasn't going to leave Sanctuary without killing someone, probably more than one. In the end I'm glad that it was just Alison, Sam and Jack rather than someone I've spent the last decade helping raise."

I shook my head, fists clenched. "Alison didn't deserve that and I can't believe you're dismissing her death so easily."

"Who should have died in her place then, Adri? You, me? Someone was going to die, that was the only outcome left us by the choices that had led us to where we were at that moment. Alison has been supporting Sam for years. On some level, whether she knew it or not, she enabled his treachery. In our world, those kinds of actions have consequences."

It was like I'd been doused in cold water. The anger was still there, but it wasn't at the forefront of my being like it had been before. If I'd had any doubts they were gone now. How could Alec possibly see the error of his ways when everyone around him held the same kind of callous beliefs?

I found myself retreating into the safety of the formality that had characterized most of my previous exchanges with Donovan.

"Could you please ask Alec if he's able to see me?"

If the abrupt change in tracks threw Donovan for a loop, he didn't show it.

"I'm sure he'll drop whatever he's working on. I'll go let him know you're here."

I watched a tiny bird with curiously bright markings jump from one flower to another while I waited. A few seconds later Alec came around the corner and joined me in front of the manor.

"Adri, I'm so glad you came by. You haven't been returning my calls and I was worried. I would have come by your house, but I didn't know if that would get you in more trouble with your mom. Didn't you get any of my messages?"

"I got them; I just didn't think it was a good idea to call you back."

"I'm really sorry about what I said. You didn't deserve that."

I pulled my phone out of my pocket and handed it to him. "Here, this is yours."

He looked at the phone, turning it over in his hands for several seconds. "Adri...we had a fight. A fight that took place right after we'd both been in the most stressful situations of our lives. Neither of us was thinking very clearly."

I interrupted, shaking my head slowly. "This isn't about our fight. Mom decided to move us away from Sanctuary."

"You don't have to go. We'll get you legally emancipated. If that doesn't work, I'll arrange for you to be kidnapped. You could disappear until you're eighteen. You can stay, I want you to stay."

I nodded. "I'd like that, I really would, but it won't work. My mom needs me. More than that, you need to understand that I'm leaving because of what you allowed to happen, not just while Agony was here, but before. You have the ability to be a great leader, but you're not going to realize that, not unless something makes you understand what you give up by treating people like they are property."

Alec shook his head. "We had a fight; we're having a fight, even. Don't run away. I love you, I really do."

"I hope you do. If you really do love me then maybe this will be the wakeup call you need. Don't try to stop me, don't call me, don't swing by for a visit. We're over."

I turned around and walked away but not before three scenes burned themselves into my memory.

Jess and Isaac. She looked scared and lost, a stranger in a world where everyone she met knew more about her than she did. Isaac looked so very alone. He had lost the person who most understood him and in her place was a stranger he felt obligated to take care of.

Jasmin had been standing partially hidden by a tree, but even with the foliage obscuring most of her face I could all but read her mind. She'd hurried to Ben's house the night Alison had died, but Agony had kept us all too late. Ben was gone, probably for good, and he would spend the rest of his life craving a high she'd never be able to satisfy again.

Jess, Isaac and Jas were bad enough, but it was the sight of Alec that nearly ripped my heart out of my chest. He'd stood strong while Brandon tried to kill his friends and family. He'd never even flinched when Agony was within centimeters of triggering the fight that would have destroyed us all. He was so strong, but now he looked like I'd hollowed him out and left a robot where his heart used to be.

I forced myself to keep walking. I made it all the way back to the Jeep before I broke down. As we drove away I tried to tell myself I'd done the right thing. I wasn't sure anymore though. All I knew was Alec wouldn't forgive me. Right or wrong, there wasn't any going back.

Author's Note

To be honest, as I write this I'm a bit nervous about how Splintered will be received. On the one hand I'm a writer. On the other hand, I'm a fan of Alec and Adri's story—I guess really the very first fan. As a writer this was exactly where the story needed to go, and I'm not sure that I've ever managed to write something this powerful before now. As a fan, I'm positively broken up about where Adri left things, and knowing what comes next for them doesn't make things any easier.

Fan-Dean, who happens to be a hopeless romantic, wants all of you fellow fans to know that the ride will be worth it. We've got a couple of other things we need to go see before we get where all of you want to go next, but those stories are part of what Writer-Dean knows needs to happen before Alec and Adri can continue their journey.

If you've enjoyed, Broken, Torn, and Splintered please help spread the word. Every tweet, blog post, review and recommendation to a friend is immensely helpful and greatly appreciated. Also please consider signing up for my mailing list. I will only use it to announce new releases.

Intrusion

(Part of Jessica's Story)

I hadn't felt quite right for a couple of days now. Then again, my memory was something measured in days rather than months and years like it should have been. What did I really know when it came to 'normal'? Ever since I'd lost my memory, I'd felt out of place, like I didn't really belong with Isaac and the others. The feeling had gotten worse as time had gone on, rather than wearing away like everyone had been telling me it would. It was starting to make me worried.

It finally got bad enough that I decided to brave Alec's presence to ask if I could go into town. I found him in his studio, surrounded by empty canvases, a brush in his hand, apparently unable to bring himself to start on his next painting. He looked up as I walked into the studio, and he even mustered a smile, but it left me feeling like the effort had cost him more than it should have. It was like it had pulled on a wound that wasn't healing quite right, one that had started bleeding again just because I'd been selfish enough to pierce his sanctuary.

He didn't say anything, so I cleared my throat, gave him a second or two to tell me to get lost, and then launched into my petition.

"Sorry, Alec. I know you've said I still have a lot to learn, but I'd really like to go into town. Just for a couple of hours. Everyone has been cooped up at the estate ever since Adr...I mean for days."

He flinched a bit when I almost let her name slip out, but nodded. "That's fine—Dom tells me that you're doing much better with regards to your control. As long as Isaac is fine taking you into town, I have no issues."

There it was again. "I'd really like to go by myself. I mean I don't want to bother Isaac. He shouldn't have to take me everywhere like I'm some kind of kid who needs babysat all of the time."

Alec set his brush down. "I don't think that Isaac views accompanying you as a chore, and I really don't think that you're ready to be out without someone around to help make sure that you don't let your true nature slip out into the open."

My nature. It made it sound like a curse, but that actually wasn't too far off of how it felt most of the time. Every adolescent boy in the world would have loved to be able to do what I could do, what we could do, but so far the downsides were outnumbering the cool bits by about eighty to one.

"I—I'm happy to go with someone, I'd just rather it not be Isaac right now."

Actually I didn't want to go with anyone. I was the very bottom of the pack, which meant that no matter who I was with, I'd pretty much have to jump on command. Everyone meant well for the most part, but our beasts made life hell in a lot of ways. Only having a very strictly defined hierarchy kept us from dealing with constant dominance fights.

It still made for plenty of posturing, but it helped a little. Frankly I'd have been much worse off if it wasn't for Isaac. Although James and Jasmin seemed to trade up positions on an almost hourly basis, Isaac was clearly the most powerful wolf after Alec, and he'd made it clear to everyone, Alec included, that there would be no subjecting me to the kind of crap most packs routinely dished out to their submissives.

It rankled a little bit to know that Isaac was the only reason my life wasn't even worse than it already was. Knowing he had that kind of control over me, that he could revoke his protection at any moment if he felt so inclined, was hard to deal with. Even harder was the way that he looked at me when he thought I wouldn't notice. He was in love with me still. Only I wasn't that person anymore. Which meant he wasn't really in love with me; he was in love with a memory.

"Okay, if you can find another member of the pack who's willing to go with you, who's willing to risk Isaac's displeasure when he finds out that you left without him, I'm not going to interfere."

I nodded and retreated out of Alec's studio.

Going to Rachel probably could have been construed as cheating. She was part of the pack, there was no doubting that, but she was a normal human, so in theory she was even lower on the food chain than I was. Only the fact that Alec was quite literally willing to kill to protect his sister allowed her to be something more than an errand girl.

"Hi, Jess. How are things?"

"Honestly? I think I might go frickin stir crazy if I have to stay cooped up at the estate much longer. I just talked to Alec and he said if I could find someone willing to go with me, that I could go into town. Are you up for it?"

"Careful, neither Donovan nor your dad would be thrilled to hear you saying that kind of stuff."

The response was habit, habit and an attempt to buy some time to think. Rachel was younger than the rest of us, but she wasn't a dummy. She'd had plenty of time to get a handle on the politics and positioning that were an inherent part of pack life.

Those two things would have made her cautious all by themselves, but she also had a firm understanding of just how much Alec had stuck his neck out on her behalf. It made her very careful not to do things that would cause him trouble.

"Please. It's not like I'm really saying anything for them to get excited about." James had taught me pseudo swear words as a way to nettle Isaac. I knew it, and I knew I shouldn't be using them just to spite Isaac, but sometimes I couldn't help myself. He was so proper, and there really were occasions that called for expressions that had a bit more oomph to them than the dry, proper stuff that Donovan, Rachel and Alec's butler and surrogate father, was so fond of.

Rachel rocked back slightly on her heels and then looked up and met my eyes. "You're not planning on telling Isaac, are you?"

I'd thought about not telling her the truth, but I had few enough allies in this crazy house. I couldn't afford to piss one of them off.

"Not if I can avoid it. If I tell him I'm leaving he'll come along, but it's him I need to get away from the most."

Rachel's sigh was a heavy thing. "I know this is tough for you, Jess, but Isaac really is a great guy. He's just trying to look out for you."

"I know. Part of me is thankful that he's running interference with Jasmin and the rest, but it's just too creepy to see him looking at me all of the time."

"Okay. I'll go with you, but we're only going to Sanctuary. It's safe enough even though the shopping utterly sucks. Oh, also I'm bringing my homework."

I felt a smile tug at the corners of my mouth. Rachel had the kind of cheery, bright personality that you couldn't help but respond to in kind.

A few minutes later we were in my SUV, headed at a leisurely pace into the biggest city I remembered ever actually being in. The thought just begged to be asked.

"Hey, Rach. Have I ever been to a real city?"

"Depends on what you call real. We've been to Vegas a few times. As far as shopping goes, it's about as good as anywhere else you're going to find in the States."

"Never a really big city though? New York, DC, LA?"

I caught her headshake out of the corner of my eye. "No. At least not the first two. Everything east of the Mississippi is off limits, so I know you've never been to either of those two. You might have been to LA, but if so it was one of the pseudo-secret missions. Alec occasionally sends people off to manage some deal or another, and usually I don't know much more than that they were gone for a few days."

Hmm, that was something new. My world had been limited to the estate and one trip into town ever since I could remember. With everything being off limits, I'd never actually stopped to think about there being different levels of forbidden.

"What's the deal with the east?"

Rachel paused for a second, waiting until I'd finished pulling into the parking spot across from the park.

"It's a combination of two things really. The east has the highest population density in the entire country. When you put that many people into such a small area vampires are a natural byproduct."

"Wait. Vampires? Like suck-your-blood, cheesy, fanged guys with bad hair?"

Rachel shook her head. "No, like immortal parasites who we've managed so far to mostly keep unaware of our existence."

It was a lot to process, but based on the way that Rachel was avoiding meeting my eyes now, I was pretty sure that wasn't the end of it.

"Okay, Rach. Spill it."

"So the vampires are bad enough, but the other reason we aren't allowed out to the East Coast is the Coun'hij."

I felt a shudder work its way from my center out to my shoulders. It had been the Coun'hij, one of them at least, who had taken away my memories. All I remembered from that night was waking up in the cavern below the estate surrounded by the pack, all of whom were bruised and bloodied.

That didn't count, of course, the three pack members who had been killed that night. Part of me wasn't interested in pursuing this particular topic with Rachel, but the rest of me was absolutely driven to know everything I possibly could about my tormentors.

"Okay so I get the vampires bit. They don't know about us so they don't come after us, which is probably a good thing since if they are anything like the popular culture version they could reproduce at some pretty alarming rates. Why does the Coun'hij care though?"

Rachel's shrug was almost an apology. "I'm not really sure. There are a few theories running around. The Coun'hij isn't exactly popular with the various packs, so it's entirely possible that they are just trying to keep their base of operations secret."

"Right, except they don't need to feel threatened by the rest of us. The guy who ripped my memories out of my head isn't even very high up their ranks. What could the other packs possibly do to a group that powerful?"

"Don't overestimate them, Jess. They're the scariest thing our people have had to deal with in several centuries, but that doesn't make them unbeatable. Half of their advantage is that they always get to pick the timing of every confrontation. All it takes is one or two hybrids manifesting a truly powerful ability and deciding not to throw their lots in with the Coun'hij. That and the ability to pick our own time and place."

"Is that what Alec was planning on doing?"

I was definitely into forbidden topics now. Looking in as an outsider, more or less, it was easy to see the scars in the pack dynamic that our decade-long standoff with the neighboring pack had left. Everything I'd been able to tease out of Isaac or the others sounded pretty bleak.

The rival alpha, Brandon, *had* manifested a really uber ability, and all of the smart money had us ending up as goners sooner rather than later since nobody on our side was even remotely in that class. We'd been outnumbered, and outmuscled.

That had all changed the night that Alec had been backed into a challenge match with Brandon. Out of nowhere Alec had finally manifested an ability, and it had been a game-changer. Draining your opponent's energy from several yards away didn't sound like anything to get that excited about, but the visual Isaac had described flat gave me chills.

Both packs had collapsed to the ground, the next best thing to lifeless corpses waiting to be dealt with. The effect had been temporary, and once Alec stopped sucking everyone dry it was only a matter of time before our natural vitality took over and people started moving around again. Still, the whole pack had been convinced that we had it made. The next time we got into trouble, we'd just expected Alec to flip the switch on his pocket nuke. Game over.

Only it hadn't worked out that way. Instead it hadn't come when called, and the pack had paid the price of not giving the Coun'hij what they wanted.

I debated trying to probe a little more, but it wasn't worth the potential trouble. Alec wasn't telling anyone much of anything where his power was concerned. Nobody was talking about it, but it was an open secret among the pack that once the rest of the world decided that we didn't have a magic bullet anymore, things were going to get rough.

I shook my head and followed Rachel over to the closest bench.

"You're sure you're fine to just sit here, Jess? I mean, I know it's not really the ideal time away from the estate, but I'm way behind."

"It's okay. Mostly I just wanted out. Sitting, walking, doesn't much matter as long as I get a break. Besides, the park really is pretty."

I said it more to soothe Rachel's worries than out of a real appreciation for the park, but as I looked around I realized it was the truth. We were on the side of town that tended more towards greenery, and the park was a beautiful example of landscaping. Semi-wild roses grew off to one side of the space, somehow pulling the eye away from the periphery and leading it to the center where a simple stone sculpture effortlessly dominated the slight elevation upon which it was located.

Visually everything was perfect, but it would have still been incomplete without the stream opposite the roses. The sound as the water tumbled across the rocks formed the perfect auditory complement.

I watched the sunlight dance across the surface of the water for several minutes and then finally sat down next to Rachel on the bench. The warm metal slowly pulled the tension out of my knotted shoulders, and I felt my eyes closing.

I was nearly to the point of nodding off when the breeze carried over the foulest scent I'd ever run across. My eyes snapped open as my heart rate shot up. Rachel looked up from her book and then went completely still as her mind registered my distress.

"What is it, Jess?"

"I'm not sure. A smell—a bad one."

Maybe someone else would have disregarded something as simple as a scent, but even just a few weeks had been enough to teach me that for a shape shifter our sense of smell was one of the most important warning systems we had. Rachel had been part of the pack long enough that she already knew stuff I was still trying to learn.

"Can you describe it?"

"Something stale, maybe iron."

"Old blood with a hint of decay?"

I felt my eyebrows climb as I realized Rach had hit on it exactly. "You can smell it too?"

Rachel was on her feet already, pulling me up. My beast surged up at her presumption, but we both knew she outranked me. I let her pull me towards my car, still a bit confused. Once I was moving under my own power she let me go and flipped out her phone.

"We've got vampires in the area."

Alec's response had none of the fuzzy distance I'd been picking up from him ever since Adri had left.

"How do you know? Did you see them?"

"No, but Jess smelled something odd—the description sounds like what you told everyone to be on the lookout for."

There was a pause as Alec ran through decision trees. "Okay, don't go home. If you've been spotted we don't want to lead them back here. Head to the center of town, find as big a crowd as you can and just stay put until we show up. When we drive past follow us."

My heart was still frantically hammering away inside my chest as we pulled away from the curb. I wanted nothing more than to just stomp on the gas, but Rachel kept reminding me not to do anything to attract attention.

The center of town wasn't any more or less deserted than usual, but it felt like there weren't nearly enough people to serve as a shield if worse came to worst. Rachel finally pointed at a small restaurant with an outdoor patio which had a cop car parked in front of it and I carefully pulled in behind it.

As we sat waiting for Alec and the rest of the pack, I found that I was getting more anxious not less. It only took a moment's thought to know exactly why. Rachel had her phone out and looked like she was texting, but I couldn't not ask.

"How does it work? I mean fighting as wolves. I've barely transformed since the Coun'hij was here, and I've never fought with Dom or Jas."

Rachel's eyes got big, but she waited to respond until she'd finished her text. "That was a bad idea, Jess. You know what pack life is like. I know you're towards the bottom of the food chain here, but you still need to be able to protect yourself. Otherwise you're just relying on Isaac even more to protect you from the inevitable squabbling."

"I...I guess I hadn't thought about it that way. I went and watched everyone spar one of the first times right after everything happened. I'd been planning on participating, but it was scary the way everyone was going at each other."

"That's because they all know their lives depend on how well they can protect themselves. If anything the fighting was probably more intense because of the Coun'hij having just been there. Even so, they would have been careful with you. Isaac or Alec either one would have been able to control their beasts enough to teach you rather than just ripping into you."

I suddenly felt really stupid. "I guess I didn't think of it that way. I was just thinking about how much it was going to hurt and worrying about what would happen if Isaac couldn't rip Jas off of me fast enough once I'd lost."

Her phone chirped but she ignored it. "It's water under the bridge now, but you have to remember that there's still so much you don't know yet. If Alec or Isaac asks you to do something, they'll have thought it through. Frankly I'm surprised that Alec let you bow out. I'd have expected for him to push the issue."

"He tried, but Isaac got in his face about it."

The look on Rachel's face pulled at my heart. It wasn't just sad, it was nearly hopeless. I almost asked what was wrong, but it didn't take a rocket scientist to figure out what was bothering her. Alec had kept his position at the top of the pack in no small part because Isaac invariably backed him to the hilt. With everything that had happened when the Coun'hij had come, it wasn't surprising that Alec had lost some real goodwill with the rest of the pack.

I cleared my throat. "I'm sorry, Rach. I don't mean to make things worse for Alec. I really do believe he's doing the best he can for us."

"It's not your fault. I get how scary all of this must be for you. It's just that everyone but Alec has been so focused on trying to avoid being killed by Brandon and the others that it's like they're operating blind now. From the way everyone is turning on each other you'd think we were out of the woods, but if anything we're in more danger now than we were before."

"Because of the dispossessed?"

"Yeah, they top the list. If we're at the point where even Isaac isn't thinking things through, then what's to stop one of them from coming in and taking over? No dispossessed can come in and defeat a healthy pack, but there are so many of them. Once word gets out that a pack is starting to disintegrate a steady trickle of them will come through looking to topple Alec."

"Right, but Alec's one of the best fighters around. Everyone says so."

"They'll wear him down. Without his power that's all he is, a good fighter. Sooner or later someone will get lucky, or someone will force a challenge when he's hurt. If the pack won't lay everything on the line to protect him it's only a matter of time."

It was stuff that had been nibbling away at the back of my mind for a few days now, but it was different hearing Rachel lay out the future in such stark detail. I opened my mouth, not sure what I was going to say, when it struck me that I hadn't once thought about Andrew.

"Rach, what about my dad? I mean right now. There are vampires in the area and Alec's about to leave Dad, Donovan and your mom all by themselves."

She reached out and squeezed my hand.

"I know. It's a bit scary, but I expect Donovan is helping all of them plus James' mom down into the vault. Alec wouldn't have left them alone, even protected by the vault, if there was any other option."

Relief washed over me, not just because Andrew was going to be okay, but because Rachel hadn't seemed to judge me for not thinking of him sooner. She'd probably thought of her mom first thing. For me it still wasn't second nature to think of the old man in the wheelchair as someone I loved. Probably because I didn't. Not yet. He was such a nice old man that I was pretty sure I'd come to love him, but for now he was just as much of a stranger to me as everyone else currently in my life.

I looked up at the rear-view mirror and breathed a sigh of relief when I saw James' Honda and Jasmin's Mercedes headed towards us. I dropped the Escalade back into gear and followed them to the high-school parking lot.

Isaac, James, and Dom all exited their vehicle at the same time that Rach and I jumped down out of the Escalade. Jasmin swung her door open, but neither she nor Alec made any move to get out as the rest of us clustered around the Mercedes.

Alec didn't look up from his phone, but as soon as we were all assembled he started firing off questions at me.

"How many of them did you smell, and where were you two when you smelled them?"

I opened my mouth to respond and then felt my face flush as I realized I'd been so panicked that I hadn't even tried to gather the most basic intelligence on what we were about to face. Rachel patted me on the side and then stepped closer to the car.

"We were at Monument Park, Alec. That's really about all we know."

He tapped his screen a few more times and then shook his head. "We need more to go on than that, Rach. You're not doing Jess any favors by sheltering her right now. Jess, how old did the scent smell?"

"I...I'm not really sure. It seemed old, but that might have been more of the nature of the scent itself. Like old blood."

I felt more than heard a low rumble and realized that Isaac hadn't appreciated Alec's tone with me. I mentally sat on the inclination to bristle at Isaac's reaction, but I hated the fact that I did actually need his protection.

Alec nodded at something on his screen and then took a deep breath. "Okay, here's how this is going to go down. Rachel, you're going to drive Jess's car. The rest of us will go out on foot in two-man teams, Isaac and Jess on one side, James and Dom on the other, Jas and I in the center."

My insides tightened up at the thought of being out on one edge of the group, but it made sense to keep Alec in the center such that he had the shortest possible distance to get to whoever ended up in trouble.

"Dom, Jess and Rachel will all be on a conference call. Jas, you'll give Rach your phone as well and she'll speaker a call with me such that if anyone finds something, the other two groups will know immediately."

Rachel nodded, but I could tell she was scared. Out of all of us, she was the least able to protect herself, but Alec wouldn't send her home alone, so she had no choice but to tag along and hope the relative safety of the vehicle proved sufficient.

Alec waited until the rest of the pack nodded and then continued. "Vampires tend to be somewhat solitary, so it's likely that we're not going to come up against more than three of them. That means we'll likely have them outnumbered, but I don't want anyone caught off guard if we end up facing a larger group for some reason."

Jasmin was starting to pace, but it wasn't nerves on her part, she was actually keyed up at the idea of facing down one of the other supernatural group of bad asses out there. I let my mind wander as I wondered if she'd been like this before Ben had left. It was a mistake; I missed part of Alec's instructions.

"...probably going to be carrying swords or some other kind of edged weapon. Work the flanks, and unless it turns out that we're outnumbered, there's no need to get in a rush about anything. We can wait until everyone arrives and we've properly tired them out. Once they get sloppy it will be relatively easy to drag them down."

Dom cleared her throat. "Alec, what of their powers?"

"We'll just have to hope these are young. A vampire usually has to be at least a couple hundred years old before their powers really become useful in a fight, and even then it requires a degree of concentration on their part, so keep the fight mobile; and if there is more than one of these parasites, make sure we don't leave any of them unoccupied."

A few minutes later Isaac and I were strolling towards the center of town. The rest of the briefing had gone more or less as I'd expected right up to the point where Alec had handed Rachel a deadly-looking semi-automatic and told her to avoid getting pulled over.

Isaac and I had been walking for several minutes before I decided to broach the subject of my unauthorized field trip. I muted my phone so Rachel couldn't hear and then cleared my throat.

"Don't take out your anger on Rachel, okay? She was just trying to be my friend."

"As if I can take anything out on Rachel. As long as Alec is determined to let the two of you act foolish, there isn't a whole lot I can do about it. Best turn the phone back on. If we get jumped there isn't going to be time to unmute it."

I shrugged, uncomfortable with Isaac's bitterness. It was simultaneously a pointed example of why Rachel was right to worry, and a reminder that I wasn't the only one who'd lost something when Oblivion had stolen my memories.

My very identity had vanished, but Isaac had lost his best friend and paramour. My loss was by far the larger, and Isaac never tried to imply otherwise, but it wasn't like this was easy on him either.

We crossed over a stream and I felt the faintest trace of the rancid stink again. I turned to say something to Isaac, but he'd caught it too.

"Tell Rachel we've got something. The others should start angling this direction."

I started relaying instructions as Isaac jumped down to the stream bank and then waded out into the middle of the water. He grabbed a stick that was floating by and held it up to his nose.

"Tell her they're upstream somewhere. The scent we're picking up is from stuff they are throwing into the water."

Rachel paused for a second after relaying my news. "Alec says that since we smelled it from the park they must be further upstream than that. He and Jas are dropping back for the cars; one of them will pick you up in five minutes, and we'll start over from the park."

Once we arrived at the park, Alec and Jas started walking upstream. The rest of us ranged out to either side while Rachel paralleled us as best as she was able from the road. The scent got more frequent and stronger the longer we were walking. When we finally rounded a corner and saw a large industrial complex Isaac shook his head and then pulled me back behind the hill.

"Should have known the bloodsuckers would choose this place."

"Is this place special somehow?"

"No, just an eyesore Alec would have had taken care of years ago if Brandon hadn't been so determined to maintain it as you see it now. Alec probably has plans to clear it out still; the Coun'hij just threw a wrench into all of his plans."

We'd been walking long enough for the sun to start to set behind us. I didn't necessarily fancy hunting vampires down in the dark, but in theory they were more sight-based than we were, so it should all even out.

Rachel pulled up slowly beside us, lights off, engine barely idling, as the rest of the pack jogged over. Alec started pulling off his clothes to reveal the stretchy ha'bit we all wore underneath our clothes. The rest of the pack followed suit as he started explaining the plan of attack. I slowly did the same. The ha'bit was better than being naked, but I still felt uncomfortable stripping down to so little around people I'd known for such a short time. Worse was the fact that I didn't feel comfortable slipping into my four-footed shape, especially not if we were about to get into a real fight.

"Jas, Isaac, James and I will go in through the front gate. Four legs and stay low and under cover as much as possible, we won't be moving super-fast. Jess, Dom, I want the two of you to circle around the right side and work your way to the back exit. It's a bit overgrown, but I don't fancy trying to run them down if they've got a vehicle and they try to break that direction. Pull the gate shut behind you, wedge it closed the best you can, and then stay there and stop them from opening it back up."

My heartbeat shot through the roof. It was bad enough when I did that with Rachel, it was worse when it happened with the rest of the pack. Unlike her, they could all hear my pulse and it was a blaring announcement of just how scared I was.

Isaac shifted slightly closer to me, the instinct to reassure me apparently at odds with his sure knowledge that I wasn't comfortable with him so close when I was the next best thing to nude.

Alec pretended not to notice and continued, turning to Rachel.

"Rach, turn the Escalade around and then lock the doors and keep the engine running. If you see them break this direction either on foot or in a vehicle honk the horn. Twice for on foot, three times for a vehicle."

I was shaking now. Not even Rachel could fail to see my terror.

"Alec, don't make Jess go, she's not ready for this."

Alec shook his head. "They shouldn't have any problems, but if they do run into a vampire, things will go much better if there are two of them. They don't have to bring it down, they just need to hold it up until the other four of us can get there."

Isaac opened his mouth, probably to protest as well, and Alec turned on him with a flare of power that set my teeth on edge.

"Don't, Isaac. I know what you're going to say, but you're reaping the fruits of your decision earlier. If you'd backed down then, we'd have worked with her before now. At worst she'd be comfortable on four legs. At best she'd be some real use in a fight."

The answering rush of power from Isaac was impressive, but still not in the same league as Alec. For the briefest of moments the decision hung in the air and then Isaac bowed his head and took a step back.

The energy bubbling off of Alec was still nearly enough to bring me to my knees. Alec opened his mouth as if to say something, but instead just pointed at Dom and me and then whipped his arm around towards the back of the complex.

I looked over at Dom, but she'd already dropped down to hands and knees, and in between one breath and the next her form rippled into that of the big cat that was her alternate form. I sucked in as much air as my lungs would hold, and then let my beast rush up from the corner of my being where I usually kept her chained.

It hurt, but in an odd kind of way that was over so quickly that I almost didn't remember the pain of the transition once it was done. For a second I just basked in the glory of being a wolf again. Every single sense was enhanced, but my top two favorites were just how incredibly sensitive my nose had become, and the way that everything had a thin film of light over top of it.

Isaac had tried to explain the theory behind why we could see a soft glow around anything living, but frankly I didn't care why, I only cared that it turned the otherwise-dull landscape into a glistening paradise. I swung my head back and forth, drinking in the beauty, and then a low growl from Alec reminded me that I was supposed to be following Dom.

I slipped off into the relative darkness. Tracking her was easy, she'd made no attempt to try and hide her scent trail, and she wasn't moving overly fast, so I caught up quickly. I'd spent as little time as possible on four feet, but now that I was gliding through the night with such ease it was hard to remember why.

Dom brushed up against me, shouldering me to one side, and I had to fight back the growl that tried to bubble up past my teeth. She was vastly more experienced at all of this than I was, but in this shape it was harder to remember those kinds of things. My beast didn't care who was most experienced, it cared who was the strongest, and we'd never had it out to see who was dominant; at least not that *I* could remember.

I stepped on the urge to launch into a full-blown dominance challenge right then and there, instead choosing to fall back enough that I could just follow her. Not being able to talk was less than convenient. It was one of the many advantages that hybrids like Alec, James and Isaac had over the rest of us. Those on four legs had to rely on body language to try and communicate. Dom had mentioned in passing her belief that lack of speech had been the primary reason that cats like her hadn't ever come out on top in the wars they'd had with the wolves.

Unlike wolves, cats seemed to get stronger and stronger as they aged. It meant that a really powerful southern shape shifter was a match singly for some of the smaller packs, but their solitary nature had so far kept them bottled up down in South America.

Dom pulled up short and I realized I hadn't been paying enough attention. We'd arrived while I'd been thinking about things that had less than zero importance to me right now. A chill worked its way up between my shoulder blades and down my muzzle.

The gate was open, and given the way the vegetation had been hacked up, it was a recent change. Dom padded up to the gate, softly batted at it and then looked pointedly at me. I bristled a little at the implication, but she was right. If one of us had to reassume our normal shape, and be less useful in a fight, it was better for me to do it.

I mentally reached out to my beast and pulled her back, cramming her back down into the corner of my being where she usually dwelt. It was a fight, but it was always a fight. Eventually I pushed her back enough that the transformation swept back through me, leaving me panting on my hands and knees.

I'd forgotten just how inconvenient it was to go back to two legs when you didn't have a pair of shoes handy. The decaying asphalt wasn't so bad at least. I pulled the gate shut without too much of a problem, but I had to walk up the fence for quite a ways before I finally found a twisted bit of metal that looked like it would serve to immobilize the gate.

Dom paced me the whole way there and back, tail slowly twitching back and forth as she watched for trouble. I bit back a curse as I stepped on a jagged branch, and then I was back on the road and wedging the gate closed.

Dom was pacing back and forth expectantly so I sank back down to my hands and knees. I had a split second to realize why I was so uncomfortable being a wolf, and then the change was upon me and I was padding along on four legs again.

It was the fear that this time I wouldn't be able to push my beast back down, that I'd be trapped as a wolf forever.

We didn't range very far away from the gate, just far enough for the smell of vampire to get stronger. This close I was able to start picking out some subtleties to the stench. Cigarettes, alcohol, cucumber melon lotion. There were other scents, but they were more subtle, less easily distinguished.

I felt my guts tighten up as I realized that there was more than just the one vampire we'd been hoping we were facing. Still, three vampires shouldn't be too bad. Alec and the others would outnumber their opponents. As long as none of the vampires were too old, too powerful, we'd be okay.

The barest hint of Isaac's scent cut through the vampire smell, and then there was yelling from an area halfway between us and the front gate. Dom and I both tensed up as strains of violence drifted back to us.

There was a meaty thud as someone was thrown into what sounded like the side of a dumpster, and then three sets of footsteps, moving our direction, very quickly. If I'd been by myself I probably would have crouched down and tried to go unnoticed, but Dom was already moving forward, sliding behind a stack of abandoned barrels that would serve as a decent ambush point.

My hesitation cost me. There wasn't time now to find concealment of my own, but in moving to follow Dom I'd abandoned the patch of shadow that might have otherwise sheltered me. I was stuck between two options, neither one quite close enough when the first vampire came around the corner of the rusted crane just ahead of me.

The other two were only half a stride behind him, and the trio slowed just long enough to confirm that I was by myself.

The one in the lead was a tall, dark-haired male with some kind of straight sword held loosely in his left hand. At his right was a shorter, ultra-slender, man with a pair of small axes. A redheaded woman with some kind of curved cutlass rounded out the trio.

"Liz, get the vehicle, we'll take care of this one."

Liz opened her mouth to argue, but the taller man cut her off with a hiss.

"The master can't hold the others off for forever."

I crouched and moved slightly, retaining just enough presence of mind to try and lure them more optimally past Dom's hiding spot. The woman took off again at a run, heading parallel to the fence in the opposite direction from where I'd found the rod we'd used to bar the gate.

I noticed her only peripherally, instead focusing on the two men who'd spread out slightly as they advanced on me. The fear hadn't left, not really, but it'd managed to loosen some of the control I normally kept on my beast, and she knew exactly what she wanted to do to these two.

We moved up slightly, judging the distance between us and the vampires as the first one walked past Dom. It was going to be tricky. Too close and I risked having to fight the leader before Dom had a chance to take down the short guy. Too far away and the leader would be able to turn and attack Dom before I could get there and distract him.

Time seemed to slow down slightly with multiple heartbeats between each step, and then the second man was even with Dom and she was sailing through the air. Something about the change took Dom's normally tiny frame of a hundred and fifteen pounds and turned it into a monstrous two hundred and thirty pounds. She hit the vampire with the impact of a professional linebacker and drove him to the ground as her jaws closed around his neck.

The leader had spun towards Dom as she leapt, but I darted towards him, causing him to whirl back towards me. There was a moment of decision. I could feel the vampire weigh his options. The girl was too far away to make it back in time, even assuming he was willing to call her back. He could try to save the shorter man, but Dom was definitely on top and the struggles were already starting to abate slightly.

Even assuming he could drive Dom off, there would be a period of time before the other man was back on his feet and fighting, and during that brief window, the taller man would have to face both Dom and me at once.

Between one heartbeat and the next, the vampire moved towards me, sword flickering out. I slipped to one side, narrowly dodging the strike. He was faster than I expected, and he was pressing forward without hesitation now that he was committed.

We circled, but it was readily apparent that I was outclassed, and his sword was getting closer and closer to slicing into me.

The sounds of fighting were closer now, but I didn't have much time. Out of the corner of one eye I saw Dom release her prey and head my direction. The shorter vampire wasn't dead. He was still moving, but not very quickly, so Dom and I had at least a few seconds to double-team my opponent.

One of my dodges wasn't quite fast enough and a blaze of fire kindled across my left side as the dark, lifeless steel sliced into me. Dom picked that moment to spring at the vampire, but he was faster than she expected, and she missed his neck.

I darted in, trying to get my teeth on something, but while he was retreating now, he was doing a masterful job of using the terrain to his advantage. The sword seemed almost everywhere at once, perfectly complementing the dumpsters, walls, and other bits of industrial waste he was using to help keep us at bay.

The shorter vampire barreled into Dom from nowhere. She'd apparently kept a better eye on our surroundings than I had, mostly twisting out of the way, but one of the axes still managed to connect with a glancing blow to her shoulder.

The taller vampire took a quick step towards Dom, intent on finishing off the greater threat, and I saw my opportunity. His head was protected by a mostly-collapsed roofing strut, but that wasn't my target.

I latched onto the meaty part of his sword arm and whipped him around, slamming him into a metal post before he could respond, but I didn't manage to keep him off balance. No human frame should have had the strength to jerk me around the way he was, but he was apparently old enough that the normal limits didn't apply.

I whipped my neck back and forth, trying to break his arm before letting go, but it refused to break, and I felt a mounting sense of desperation. I was fully committed, but he still had a hand free, and only the violence of my movements was keeping him from bringing it into play.

The fighting was even closer now. I caught glimpses of the action as the tall vampire and I circled. Jasmin clinching with a skeletally thin woman, James and Alec circling with a cloaked figure who impossibly seemed to be holding them at bay, Isaac squared off against two more vampires.

We were all within a couple dozen yards of each other now, but all too wrapped up with our own opponents to help each other out. I whipped my head back to the left again, and it happened. My right foreleg slipped and I failed to pull the vampire off balance.

Jasmin or Dom would have let go right then and there and sprung away, but I hesitated and the vampire pulled a knife from somewhere. I tried to correct my error, tried to get away, but he was too quick.

The feel of the knife sliding into my side brought a new meaning to the concept of terror. I thrashed around, trying to escape, but the roles had now been reversed. The vampire had me by the throat with an iron grip while his right hand dug the knife around.

I kept expecting it to pierce my heart, but ultimately it didn't matter one way or the other. I was already getting weaker. Shape shifters didn't bleed out quickly, but it was only a matter of time.

The vampire pulled the knife out, bringing his arm back so he could stab it down with more force, and then suddenly Isaac was there. The vampire tried to whirl around, but Isaac was too fast for him, sinking razor-sharp claws into the vampire's chest at the same time that he immobilized the hand holding the knife.

The realization that I was going to live occurred at roughly the same time that I finally took in the damage to Isaac's huge hybrid body. He was covered with slashes, but the most fearsome wound was created by a sword that was still sunk into his body all of the way to the hilt. On a human it would have gone through the kidneys before exiting his back, but I didn't have any idea if that was true for a hybrid as well.

Isaac looked down at me for the shortest of seconds before turning back towards the melee. By the time I pulled myself back to my feet, it was all but over. Jasmin had been finishing off her opponent at the same time that Isaac had been saving me.

Isaac's second opponent had jumped into the fray with Alec and James, pressing them quite sorely for several seconds, but Isaac had killed Dom's opponent just seconds after killing mine. Once the odds were four on two, it was only a matter of time until the vampires would be pulled down.

I watched numbly as Alec darted in and broke the master vampire's neck. I wasn't quite sure when I'd resumed human form. I absently registered the bloody state of my feet, but was in too much shock to care much.

I made it over to the rest of the pack a few steps behind Dom. Alec shrank down to his human form and shook his head as he walked over to Isaac.

"You're lucky it wasn't a couple of inches higher or you'd have bled out before you even made it to her."

Isaac's voice came out low and rough from his hybrid throat. "It was a calculated risk. On several levels."

"Calculated risk nothing. It was the kind of crazy, thoughtless thing I usually expect out of James, not you."

Isaac opened his mouth to respond, but Alec took advantage of the distraction to pull the sword free. The rush of blood nearly made me physically ill, but it was Isaac's scream that pulled most brutally at me. For a second I thought Isaac would go berserk, but instead he collapsed down onto all fours and then melted back into human form.

Alec ripped two chunks of cloth from one of the dead vampires' attire and then pulled me over to Isaac's unconscious, barely-breathing form.

"Hold this and this here and here. If we can staunch the bleeding slightly he'll be okay. Shifting forms will have repaired any really major vascular damage."

Once Alec was satisfied that I was going to keep pressure on the wounds he sent the rest of the pack forward to get Rachel and the vehicles. When James protested the order for Dom, who was obviously limping, to accompany the rest of them, Alec backhanded him into a building without even bothering to change forms.

"This is not a democracy. Dom will be fine. Just go."

Alec waited a couple of minutes after everyone else had left and then turned back to Isaac and me.

"I know you're having a hard time, Jess. It's hard on Isaac too; he just doesn't show it as much. Once upon a time you understood that. I get that things have changed, that we're all just strangers to you. Believe it or not, Isaac gets it as well."

I opened my mouth, not sure what I was going to say, but Alec shook his head and kept talking.

"There are things however that haven't changed. The most important one where you're concerned is that Isaac is still willing to run crazy risks to try and protect you. It's easy for people to say all kinds of things, but that's not Isaac. If you watch what he does, that speaks volumes and has since the two of you were little."

Scent of Tears

(Many years before Broken and Torn)

Shawn shifted around restlessly in the SUV's passenger seat. The flight in from Chicago had landed early that morning and he and his nanny, Sarah, had been on the road ever since. It was bad enough for normal kids to sit for hours. For a shape shifter like Shawn, it was almost torture; especially in his person shape. He spent almost as much time as a wolf as he did on two legs, the form he was wearing now. In fact, if his dad hadn't been so strict about his homework, he probably would've spent every hour he wasn't in school running around on four legs. Shawn checked the clock one last time before turning to Sarah.

"Are we almost there? I waited thirty minutes like you told me to."

Sarah slid a few strands of wispy gray hair back behind her ear and nodded. "You're right. I did say you could ask again. We're actually just about to turn into the lane."

Shawn sat up straighter in his seat, straining to see the large gate signifying the start of the family's country estate. True to Sarah's word, a few moments later they were driving down the one mile lane to the house. As soon as the car rolled to a stop Shawn jumped out and raced around to help Sarah out of the car.

It wasn't his favorite thing to do, but at her age if he didn't help it would take three times as long. The sooner she was settled in the house the sooner he could shift forms and go out exploring. They hadn't been out to the estate in nearly a year, and last time he hadn't been allowed out from under Sarah's watchful gaze. This year his father had agreed he could go out on his own for a couple hours at a time as long as he stayed on their property.

Sarah seemed to take hours to get her small bag out of the back of the vehicle, and then days to walk up the stairs. Shawn raced back and forth between the car and the house several times before she finally unlocked the door.

He shot up the stairs, put his toothbrush in the bathroom, his clothes in the dresser and then knelt so he could melt into his wolf form.

He looked himself over as he padded past the mirror on the bathroom door.

Black and brown fur, check. Sharp pointy teeth, check. Big ears that could hear Sarah's heartbeat all the way downstairs? Check. A wonderfully sensitive nose that was busy sampling a hundred times more smells than he'd been able to register just minutes before? Check.

The nose was almost the best part of being a shape shifter. The only thing better was how strong and fast he was. Out in the forest he could run for hours and nothing but another shape shifter could catch him.

Unfortunately, inside was a different matter. The hallway's slick hardwood was surprisingly hard to navigate as a wolf. He walked with exaggerated care, trying to avoid falling into the wall and then found himself at the top of the stairs. His dad and Sarah both climbed up and down stairs like pros, but he still fell down about as often as not.

Sarah said it just took practice, that in a couple of years stairs would be easy in both forms, but for now it was harder than it looked. Shawn carefully started down the stairs, moving in a kind of sideways hop that'd more or less worked for him before.

He actually made it two-thirds of the way down before a misstep sent him sprawling.

Sarah shook her head at him as she came around the corner from the hall that led to her room.

"If you'd just slow down, Shawn, things would go much easier."

Shawn whined and nosed the door. That was the only part of being a wolf that was worse than being a human. Without words you had to rely entirely on other things to communicate what you wanted, and Sarah was a past master at pretending not to understand him.

"Your father did say it would be ok for you to go out on your own, but you're to be back by nightfall. There's to be no hunting, and you're not to leave the estate."

A quick tail wag and rolling over onto his back served to convince Sarah of his sincerity. She opened the door and Shawn shot out in a blur. He tore across the porch and jumped down to the lawn, completely ignoring the pesky stairs.

It was heaven. The foliage flashed by in a blur his human eyes would've been hard-pressed to follow. Slowing down slightly, Shawn angled towards one edge of the estate as he tested the wind for rabbits.

The boundary wasn't marked by a fence or any of the other things humans usually chose to define the edges of their territory. Instead their family had chosen to leave it open so that animals could come and go freely. It meant there was plenty of game around, but he had to rely on the irregular strop markings his dad's claws had left on the trees to tell him when he arrived.

A few minutes later, the urge to run at least temporarily satisfied, Shawn slowed to a stop and put his nose to the ground. The smell of rabbit was incredibly strong.

Shawn picked out the most recent scent trail and followed it along the forest floor. Under trees, around rocks, and through brambles so tight it felt like they were going to rip his coat right off. The rabbit had been careful. It never exposed itself for more than a brief second, bounding from one bit of cover to the next in a flash nearly as fast as Shawn could achieve.

Shawn followed the sneaky rabbit for more than twenty minutes before the trail disappeared into a burrow. He nosed around and briefly considered trying to widen the hole enough to get more than just his muzzle in, but it was hard work and he was pretty sure the warren was too deep to dig up.

After he finally abandoned the effort, Shawn continued along the edge of the estate. His stomach starting to growl, he'd nearly decided to turn around and head back for something to eat when his nose caught the barest glimmer of a new scent.

It was like nothing he'd ever smelled before. Not sweet necessarily, but flowery-delicious and somehow it made the other scents sharper. He was already at the edge of the estate but couldn't bring himself to leave without investigating something so amazing.

A quick search turned up a stream just close enough to the border of their property for Shawn to claim he hadn't realized it was forbidden. Halfway between the stream and his current location was a muddy slope that would serve quite nicely.

Shawn ran towards the slope and then let his legs slip out from under him as he started downhill. He slid and rolled down the last half of the muddy hill, ending up at the bottom in a muddy heap exactly as planned. Sarah wouldn't be able to blame him for wanting to go wash up.

The stream was colder than expected, but it washed the mud off just fine. He splashed around for a couple of minutes and then started swimming upstream, confident there'd be no scent trail to tip Sarah off to his having left. As long as he came back onto their land at exactly the same point where he'd jumped into the stream she'd think he really had just washed off and then gone back home.

A brisk fifteen minute swim did the trick to hide his scent and then Shawn found a spot where the bank wasn't too steep and raced off looking for the scent.

He soon discovered a large, natural rock wall. The smell seemed to be coming from somewhere further ahead, so rather than trying to figure out a way to climb it, he ran along it.

The wind was sometimes deceptive. Half an hour later he realized he'd gone much further off their land than he'd meant to. His conscience finally kicked in, but just before he decided to turn back he heard them.

Hunting dogs. Judging by the howling there were at least four, and they were definitely behind him. He was stronger and faster than even most full-grown dogs, but he'd never been in a fight before, not in either form.

His heart racing, Shawn continued running, only now he started curving around away from the rock wall. It was dangerous; the wind would be carrying his scent back to them, so rather than having to track him, they could just head straight to him. Still, he had to get far enough away from the wall to use his superior speed and endurance.

The run was a nightmare. Undergrowth that had seemed to slide out of his way before, now tore at his fur, trying to slow him down. He'd expected the dogs to gain on him, but not this rapidly. Every time he slowed down to catch his breath he could feel them getting closer.

A single misstep was all it took to tilt things further against him. He was jumping over a rosebush and landed on a thorn. The needle-sharp point pierced the pad on his right foreleg, and then he was limping.

Each step was agony, the dogs getting closer by the minute. He was now headed directly away from the outcropping though, so the wind was no longer in their favor.

Shawn jumped a tiny trickle of water, likely a tributary of the stream he'd used earlier, and ducked under a pair of fallen trees. He was halfway through to the other side when he heard the hunter.

A stray breeze brought the scent of gun oil and cleaner. A person by themselves wasn't a threat to a shape shifter, but a rifle made all the difference. Nobody could outrun a bullet.

He's waiting for me. He doesn't know what the pack found, but he knew I'd be trying to get further away from the steep rock wall.

The dogs were getting closer. They had their noses down so they could track his scent but, every so often one would look up and howl.

Shawn felt his muscles trembling. He was caught between two unbeatable opponents with only minutes before one or the other would find him.

He'd nearly given up hope when the hunter slapped the arm holding the rifle. Shawn took advantage of the momentary distraction provided by the mosquito to slip away.

Running was harder now. He was starting to get tired and his paw still hurt. The blood trail he was leaving made it even easier than normal for the dogs to track him. His only hope now was to make it back to the stream.

He was shaking and cold by the time he finally heard the low gurgle of flowing water. He jumped between a couple of tall ferns and landed with all four legs paddling furiously. The dogs were only a minute or two behind and he needed to be out of sight before they arrived.

The current wasn't very strong but he made good time, he was several curves away by the time the dogs came to the end of the trail, yelping as they slid down the bank and fell into the stream. Fifteen minutes later the barking had faded into the distance.

Shawn finally worked his way back over to the bank and collapsed, wet and tired on the muddy ground. He wanted so badly to close his eyes and sleep but there was still a chance the dogs would work their way downstream looking for him.

He pulled himself back onto his paws, freezing as a new scent registered in his sensitive nose.

Another person. Maybe my age, and traces of something else, something bigger that I've never run into before.

Shawn nearly turned and ran away, but something about the smells pulled him forward, limping on his hurt paw. He finally found her down at the bottom of a sinkhole at the edge of the stream. She'd smelled hurt even from a distance, and now he could see why.

She'd somehow managed to fall and knock herself unconscious. Her lips were turning blue, but even more alarming was the way the sinkhole was slowly filling with water, threatening to swallow her.

A low whine escaped his throat. The sinkhole was too deep for him to jump out in his wolf form even unencumbered. He briefly considered jumping down and then changing back to a person, but he wasn't nearly as strong in that form. Trying to climb up the walls one handed wasn't likely to work.

Shawn's mind whirled as he tried to come up with a plan. Sarah would be strong enough to help but there wasn't time to go back, explain why he'd been outside of the estate, and bring her all the way back. He was fast, but the water was rising too quickly.

The distant sound of the hunter's dogs finally helped a plan form inside his mind. It was risky. He spent a couple of seconds trying to come up with something better and then turned and headed back towards the hunter.

Every step hurt and the smell of dogs and gunpowder ahead filled him with dread, but he kept on, creeping closer and closer until he was only a few feet from the nearest panting canine.

Shawn took a deep breath and then charged out into the clearing. He bowled over the hunting dog and then turned so he could sprint back towards the injured girl. He nearly wasn't fast enough. He'd never expected the hunter to react so quickly.

A shot rang out before he made it back to cover, ripping through the air a few feet from his head. The dogs were close on his heels, and with the way he was limping he wasn't sure he was still fast enough.

The question was answered a few seconds later when a big German Shepherd got close enough to lunge at him. The barest whisper of sound alerted Shawn to the attack and he dodged to the right just in time. The dog missed him by a couple of inches.

The hunter apparently decided against taking another shot at him with the dogs so close, but Shawn could hear the man panting as he gave chase several yards back.

The yards between him and the unconscious girl rolled by with alarming speed and after dodging another couple of attacks Shawn found himself within sight of the sinkhole. Another of the dogs was within a few feet of him now.

Shawn suddenly spun around, grabbing the larger dog by the back of its neck and flipping it towards the sinkhole.

The dog yelped in surprise as it sailed through the air. For a second it looked like Shawn's plan wouldn't work. The other dog righted himself midair, but landed with too much momentum and slid into the sinkhole, disappearing with another yelp of astonishment.

Shawn couldn't wait around, he sprang into the water again, and swam downstream as the other dogs came barreling into view. Two of the pack stopped to investigate their barking comrade, the last jumped into the stream to follow.

The pursuing dog seemed to be a better swimmer and was steadily gaining. They'd made it a hundred yards downstream before a shrill whistle from the hunter called the dog off.

Shawn wanted to lie down and give into his exhaustion, but he had to make sure the hunter was going to help the girl. He waited until the dog was out of sight and then swam over to dry land and started back upstream.

He'd only thought he'd been quiet before. Now he moved incredibly slowly, taking care not to disturb even the smallest twig. It seemed like hours passed, but finally after a few minutes he'd advanced far enough to see the sinkhole.

He almost let out an audible sigh of relief when he saw all four dogs huddled around the hunter who'd just finished carrying the girl up to ground level.

"Hush you," scolded the hunter. "We've got to get her to a hospital and I don't need the four of you jumping up on me the whole way back to the truck."

The hunter wrapped the girl in his large down coat and headed directly away from the stream. Shawn sat motionless for several minutes after the people and dogs had disappeared before finally rolling back onto all four paws and limping over to the stream.

The swim back upstream wouldn't be any fun. The journey back home on three paws would be even worse. Still, there was a pretty good chance Sarah wouldn't realize anything unusual had happened.

Author's Note

As I write this note, Alec and Adri's world has grown to include eleven published titles with another four novels to be released in the next eight months. Things are chugging along at quite the pace now, but back when I wrote the original two threads that make up this story, only Broken, Torn and Splintered had been released.

Numb (the story you're about to read) actually came about because I had the chance to join in a multi-author promo and agreed to write a short story to be posted on a website along with several other writers. Back then Alec and Adri's breakup was still very raw, and I felt like I needed to explore that more than I'd been able to in Intrusion and Trapped.

I sat down to write, and got some unexpected surprises along the way. I knew that Alec was hurting, but I hadn't realized just how difficult it was for him to not be able to confide in any of his pack mates. I knew that Adri and Cindi had been best friends as well as sisters, but back then I hadn't realized how they managed to avoid all of the sibling rivalry so common in most families.

Maybe it isn't fair to call this a story. It's more like shards of glass that have been put together into something that looks like it might be the beginnings of a stained glass window. There are hints in here that speak to the driving difference between the Reflections and the Dark Reflections books, and there are some insights into both Alec and Adri. There are some surprises—like a rare glimpse into the Paige family, happy and whole—but mostly these two fragments just contain a lot of pain.

Adri deals with her pain by taking solace in a favorite memory, while Alec tries to confront his in a more direct manner, but really they are both hurting. That's okay though because trials just make our eventual victories all the sweeter.

One Memory

Adri Paige
The Paige Residence
Manhattan, New York

Okay, here goes nothing. My assignment is to write about my favorite winter memory, and some of the idiots in my class—they call it a track here—complained that they always have a hard time starting, so we're supposed to do this stream-of-consciousness thing. I guess that means I'll just write whatever comes to mind and then I'll axe anything that I don't want my teacher to see.

Sometimes it seems like the first three-quarters of my life is one long winter memory. Minnesota gets hot during the summers, but for some reason that isn't what has stuck with me. It's the cold that always comes to mind when I think of home—only I guess I can't call it home anymore.

I remember one time when we went ice-skating on this lake an hour away from our house. It was maybe the worst idea ever. The temperature hadn't made it into double digits all week, but somebody had organized this town outing there and somehow my dad heard about it.

Dad stuffed us all in the car as soon as he got home from work and we drove straight there. I think we even forgot to eat. Once we arrived, Dad rented skates for Cindi, him and me and then we went out on the ice while Mom took pictures of us.

It was cold, I mean really, really cold. The if-I-stay-out-here-too-long-I'll-die-from-exposure kind of cold. It was a ton of fun though. The ice sucked and there were only half a dozen other people out there with us. Cindi and I fell down at least twenty times but Dad just kept picking us up and brushing the snow off of us.

We were the last ones to leave the ice. Mom had even put her camera away by the time Dad finally made us go inside. It's funny though. Most of that night is just a blur of laughter and bruises, but the thing that made the biggest impression on me was the old man running the skate rental. I think it was a church-sponsored event or something, because he would have pretty much had to have been a saint to calmly stay out there waiting for us to get off of the ice.

We stumbled off of the ice and sat down next to Mom on a rickety wooden bench. The old man was there before we managed to get our skates off and he actually knelt down in the snow and helped take them off of Cindi's feet. He said something to her, and she stiffened up like she'd been hit.

She never did tell me what he'd told her, but I think it might have had something to do with me. It sounds stupid, but I caught her looking at me more than usual on the drive home. We were bundled up in a blanket in the back seat of the car with the heater going full blast and she just looked over at me and smiled.

We hadn't been getting along all that well up to that point, so that would have been odd all by itself, but there was more. It was almost like that trip was the beginning of everything changing. It was a little while after that when Cindi and I started really becoming good friends.

Before that, Dad had always been the glue that held our family together. Mom was always a little distracted, always viewing the world through her camera lens, and Cindi and I fought more than we got along, so it had always been Dad I'd been the closest to. After that, it was almost like we became a real family.

Cindi and I became best friends and then it didn't matter so much that Mom spent most of her time off in a world of her own.

I just checked my word count and I'm way far away from being done with the assignment, especially after I cut out all of the crap that I don't want anyone else to read, but I think I'm going to just leave it alone for tonight. It's past time for me to go to bed. Maybe I'll have a better idea tomorrow.

Another Memory

Doctor Goldberg
Bel Air
Los Angeles, California

The kid who walked into my office was muscular and paranoid as hell. Unfortunately that was all I really knew about him. His new patient questionnaire was on the desk in front of me, but the odds were that everything on it was a lie. It was par for the course for my clientele.

Once you started charging a couple of thousand bucks an hour, you were into people who weren't inclined to trust doctor-patient privilege very far. It wouldn't surprise me if he'd flown in from out of town on a private jet just to see me.

He was better than most though. Usually I could find half a dozen clues as to who I was dealing with, but I was coming up completely dry with him. His clothes were perfectly suited to the warm California winter that I planned on going out and enjoying as soon as our session was over.

"Why don't you come in and have a seat...Brad."

He dropped into the chair without saying anything and I suppressed a sigh. He was going to be more difficult than most.

"What brings you here, Brad?"

"Haven't you figured me out already from my questionnaire?"

I shook my head and leaned back. He was testing me, but I'd been tested before. "The questionnaire is meant to give us a starting point for further discussion, but it can't even do that if you refuse to answer it truthfully."

I got nothing more than a raised eyebrow in response to my accusation, but I waited him out.

"It's actually all the truth, Doctor."

We were on shaky ground now. I didn't want to let him get in the habit of lying to me, but he felt like the kind who would just get up and leave if I pushed too hard too soon.

"Let's ignore the questionnaire for a moment and talk about the things that are important to you."

"I'm not sure I can answer that one, Doctor. I thought I knew what was important to me, but I've acted in a way recently that would tend to overturn those beliefs."

"Okay, Brad. Let's back into the answer. You can often tell what someone values by seeing where they spend their time and money. What was the last major purchase you made?"

I would have rather gone straight to the question of where he was spending his time, but the question of money tended to be less threatening with the kind of people who made it into my office. I was right; he didn't even pause before answering.

"We just spent fifteen million on a large parcel of land that I think has major mineral deposits underneath it."

"Was that an enjoyable purchase? Did it provide you with a sense of excitement, or maybe of power?"

He rubbed his eyes and then leaned back and shook his head. Interesting. It wasn't late enough in the day for him to be tired already. It probably meant he wasn't sleeping well. Of course there were another dozen possibilities, but it wasn't the first clue that I'd recorded since he'd walked through the door. Each bit of information helped clarify what I was up against this time.

That, more than anything, was the secret to my success. I had a photographic memory and the ability to put seemingly unrelated bits of information together to arrive at the answer I needed. It really was just a matter of time. If we spent enough time together I'd eventually figure out what was causing his underlying problems.

He shook his head again and then looked at the window. "No, it was just another transaction. We've had our eye on the area for a couple of years now. Our best computer model says that there should be...let's just say that once it's developed it will pay for itself in short order. The owner of the land died a little while ago and we had the operating capital necessary to move so we approached his estate about purchasing the land."

It was another interesting tidbit. There weren't many people and organizations in the U.S. who could come up with that kind of money at the drop of a hat, but those weren't the kinds of clues that I needed.

"What about non-business purchases? What was the last thing you bought that you looked forward to?"

He shook his head. "No, that's off-limits. I'm not interested in getting into that particular discussion, I'm here for other reasons."

I leaned forward and gave him my best 'earnest concern' expression. "Brad, why are you here? I mean, why did you choose me out of everyone else you could have gone to?"

He didn't like that question either, but this time it wasn't an emotional response. He knew where I was headed. That was okay though. In many ways it was easier to deal with the really smart patients. I wouldn't have to take him all the way through my logic; he'd see it for himself without needing to be spoon fed.

"I'm here because you're the best. Even the psychiatrists who hate you agree that you're good at what you do."

I leaned back in my chair and nodded. "Exactly, which means that you have a decision to make. You can either get up and walk out of my office, or you can answer my questions. It's entirely your call, but you came here because you knew you needed help."

"Fine. The last big non-business purchase I made was a trip."

"A trip?"

He nodded and then cleared his throat. In someone else it might not have meant anything but this was the most rattled I'd seen him yet.

"Yeah. I wanted to surprise a girl so I booked a skiing trip for our families."

"By booked you mean that you had one of your people make the arrangements?"

He closed his eyes briefly as if hiding from a memory, and then shook his head. "No, I flew out to the resort one evening after she'd gone to sleep and toured it. It was amazing. Not the skiing so much, I don't know much about that, but the cabins were gorgeous."

It was the most passion I'd seen out of him yet, so I pursued the line of questioning. "Tell me about them."

"It was almost like living outside despite the cold. They had a solarium off on one side, fireplaces in every room, and the master suite was situated at the top of the cabin and had a three hundred degree view. The night I was there you could see the snowflakes drifting down onto the skylight. It was the most peaceful thing I'd experienced in a long time."

"Your families would have been okay with the two of you sharing the master suite?"

He shook his head again, seemingly still lost in the memory of his trip. "No, it wasn't like that. Her mother would have freaked out. We would have slept in separate rooms, but the layout of the cabin sparked something inside of me. When I got back home I started looking into property so that I could start building something similar."

Now was the time to pounce. He was finally relaxing. Regardless of whether or not his questionnaire was true, we were finally getting to his real issue. It had something to do with this girl. I couldn't even say for sure how I knew, but I knew. Teasing the details out of him and working through the issues might take weeks or even months still, but I finally had a target.

"What happened after that?"

"You mean after I started planning for the future? After I realized that I wanted to spend the rest of my life with her? She left. Out of nowhere, with zero warning, she packed up and left."

Brad stood up and started walking towards the door. I violated nearly every tenet of common sense and put myself between him and the exit. Something about him had made this case more important than our twenty-minute discussion could account for. He was obviously bigger and stronger than me, but I still stepped into his path and put my hand up.

"Brad, you can't leave now. We're just starting to make some progress. We need to talk about what happened."

For a second I thought he was going to hit me. He was angry enough that he was actually shaking, but he took a deep breath and shook his head instead.

"No, Doctor. I really do believe that you're the best, but that just damns me more. If being healed is going to require that I talk about what happened with her, then the cure is worse than the disease. Stand aside. I'm leaving now and you won't see me back here."

Acknowledgements

As always, thanks needs to go out to everyone that continues to provide support in dozens of different ways. When an author chooses to go the indie route, it means they absolutely rely on their fans to get the word out, and I'm very appreciative everyone that blogs, reviews, or otherwise helps put my stories on the map.

There are a few individuals who deserve special mention. Larry and Mark who faithfully read and review just about everything I write. Mimi who served as an advance reader and righted my faulty biology facts, and Cammie who was one of the early converts.

Finally, none of this would be possible without my wife Katie, who puts up with long hours from me while she does heroic work on the editing and covers.

About the Author

Dean Murray is a prolific author with dozens of titles across multiple pen names and more than half a million copies of his work currently in circulation.

Dean started reading seriously in the second grade due to a competition and has spent most of the subsequent three decades lost in other people's worlds.

Things worsened, or improved depending on your point of view, when he first started experimenting with writing while finishing up his accounting degree. These days Dean has a wonderful wife and two lovely daughters to keep him more grounded than he used to be, but the idea of bringing others along with him as he meets interesting new people in universes nobody else has ever seen drags him back to his computer on a regular basis.

Keep up to speed on Dean's latest projects at deanwrites.blogspot.com where you'll be able to find the signup form for his mailing list.

Trapped

Kristin has always been firmly grounded in reality. Trading in small-town Idaho for an Ivy-League school wasn't going to be an easy proposition and making it happen wasn't going to leave her time for unnecessary things like crushes on boys.

Kristin is about to find out that all of the creatures she thought were nothing more than myth are actually quite real. One of the worst of them is after her, an unstoppable killing machine that will chase her across a continent.

Kristin is completely out of her depth. Her one hope is a mysterious guy with dangerous skills and a dark past. He's the kind of guy that Kristin knows she shouldn't get involved with, but as their attraction grows it becomes apparent that being with him is going to require an even bigger sacrifice than she realized.

Stone Heart

Dani's new home isn't just another stopover in a long chain of places she'll never see again, it's the home of both Caine and Jerek, two guys like nobody she's ever met before. One represents the best friend she's been hungering for, and the other represents something much more.

It should be the perfect recipe for a fairytale, but Caine and Jerek live in a dark, shadowy world and one of them is hiding secrets that will change everything, secrets that relate directly to Dani.

Reborn

True love never dies.

A new arrival at Selene's high school is about to turn her entire world upside down. She's never met anyone so attractive—or so mysterious—before this, but Jace's unyielding insistence that they've known each other for decades can't be denied—not given how familiar he feels to her.

In the hidden world of gods and fairies what you don't know can get you killed faster than anything else and only those you love have any chance of saving you.

The Society

People need to be monitored, or they'll repeat the mistakes of the Desolation, a centuries-old war that killed billions of people and destroyed civilization.

Skye is part of the Society, the hi-tech, nanite-endowed group responsible for making sure that the millions of surviving people—grubbers—are confined to the ancient, decaying cities where they can be watched to ensure they aren't redeveloping the weapons technology that came so close to extinguishing life on the planet.

When the Society's monitoring programs pick up troubling developments in one of the grubber cities, Skye is ordered in to deal with the man responsible, but what—and who—she finds once she arrives will change everything.

The Greater Darkenss

Dean writing as Eldon Murphy

Something powerful is stirring in the darkness. Something so ancient that even creatures who've been alive for hundreds of years have long since discounted this new threat as nothing more than myth.

Normal humans will be caught in the crossfire, but then that's always the way of things. Geoffrey has no memory of his past life or any idea how to survive in the violent, dangerous world in which he's trapped. Despite his best efforts, he's about to find himself in the middle of a conflict that threatens to sweep away everything, and everyone he's been fighting so hard to protect.

www.ingramcontent.com/pod-product-compliance
Lightning Source LLC
LaVergne TN
LVHW091033080826
845145LV00002B/472

* 9 7 8 1 9 3 9 3 6 3 1 1 4 *